Freaks

Episode 9

Captured

J. O. Young

Freaks Episode 9 Captured

Cover Illustration by: Pixabay

Editor: Daniel Young

ISBN: 9798826530696

Freaks Series

Freaks Episode 1 The Guardian

Freaks Episode 2 The Messenger

Freaks Episode 3 The Rebel

Freaks Episode 4 The Prisoner

Freaks Episode 5 The Sacrifice

Freaks Chained
Contains Episodes 1-5

Freaks Episode 6 Uncaged

Freaks Episode 7 Abnormals

Freaks Episode 8 Dreams

Freaks Episode 9 Captured

Freaks Unleashed
Contains Episodes 6-9

"Death was coming, but it was in for a fight."

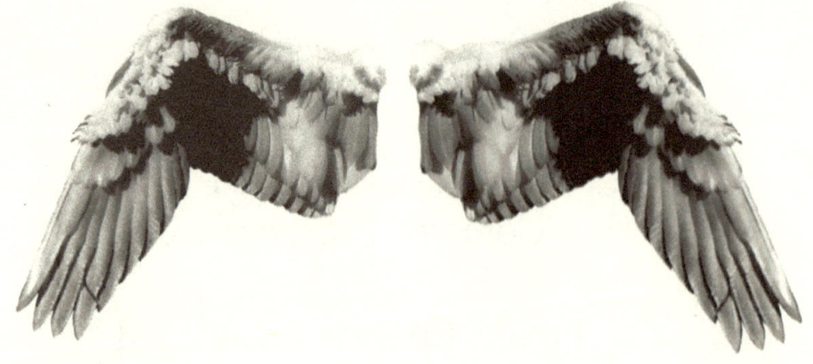

Chapter 1 Conrad

The council room was full of deep tones of gold accents throughout the walls. Even the furniture glittered with the Supreme's metal emblems. Oversized wooden chairs curved in a half circle faced a small staircase. The Supreme's throne stood at the top. The throne is a solid gold chair with an excessive amount of precious gems framing the back and legs. This is where the most critical decisions of Eurathia have been made. History has been created here. Today, hopefully, I will be able to shift those decisions in my favor. Steel slowly walked into the room and nodded. Everything was ready. Let the show begin.

Two ornate clocks chimed as the small hand clicked on the

two. The doors to the council room swung open, and all of the Fathers and Ladies that sat on the council proceeded into the room. They eyed me with curious gazes as they took their seats. The last counselor to enter was my mother. She wore a black dress that clung tightly to her until it reached the middle of her legs, then the dress flowed freely. Around her throat, she adorned a gold necklace holding several large dark blue and purple pyrope stones. Her dark black hair was swept up in a stylish bun. More blue and purple jewels accented her hair. When her gaze met mine, she froze. She gave me a small smile then sat in her chair. Once all the councilors had been seated, the doors at the top of the staircase behind the throne opened. The Supreme strolled out. He looked almost bored at the whole proceeding. He sat on the throne and then waved his hand dismissively at one of the servants standing next to him.

"This is Father Conrad," the servant announced. "He has business with the council today."

"This is the first I heard about it. The council must first approve all topics before we discuss them," one of the councilmen commented.

"I have approved this business," the Supreme announced. "Especially when this business deals directly with me."

The council nodded to the Supreme, then answered in unison, "Yes, Supreme."

"Father Conrad," the Supreme said, turning his attention to me. "You may address the council."

"Thank you, Supreme," I said as I bowed.

"There has been a malicious rumor spreading throughout the Supreme's capital that he, the Supreme himself, is a half-blood. The purpose of such deceit is to remove the Supreme from the throne. To remove a family that has dedicated their lives to serving Eurathia and pulling us from the ashes of chaos. Who would replace the Supreme? Who could fill the void of his loss?"

"If this is true, that his family is tainted, should he rule? Should a half-blood rule?" One of the councilors questioned.

"A debate and a difficult decision would have to be made if this malicious lie was true," I answered.

"Who would start such a lie?" asked a younger counselor named Fredrick.

"Who indeed?" I began. "The culprit is a conniving person who is very talented at manipulating the situation to her benefit."

"You said her," interrupted Fredrick. "Do you know who the culprit of this lie is?"

"I do," I said, shifting my demeanor from confidant to shame. "I'm afraid that it is my own mother, Lady Conrad."

A low cry of shock echoed through the room. How many, I wonder, were fake?

"Please stand, Lady Conrad, and approach," the Supreme ordered.

She smiled as she obeyed. She walked with calm confidence and grace. Lady Conrad turned her icy gaze to me. Instead of anger or betrayal, there was nothing. Her eyes were void of any emotion. She stood next to me and faced the Supreme.

"Is this true?" he asked.

"It is," she admitted.

Another murmur of shock echoed through the room. Lady Conrad spun to face the council. In that instant, she morphed from the cool, collected Lady to a passionate Eurathian.

"My fellow council, it is true. I admit that rumor started from me. But know that I didn't mean for it to spread. I wanted to wait and check my sources before I revealed the truth to you, as my son has stumbled onto the half-truth. But, we must applaud him for defending the Supreme even against his mother. I'm a proud mother for such gallantry in my child."

I smirked at her emphasis on the word child. She wanted to discredit me. I knew what she was planning to do now that I had forced her hand. All I had to do was let my mother dig her own grave.

"During this time of investigating," I questioned her. "Have you found the proof that your lie is true?"

She turned to me and patted my shoulder. "Thank you for defending the honor of the Supreme. To answer your question, I have."

"Your proof is what?" I asked.

"I have discovered that the first queen who died from poison was one of the Dragon People," she answered, looking at the council.

"Again, I ask for proof," I demanded.

"She had a child. The birth was celebrated, then mysteriously, he was missing. We all mourned his death. Then, the elder Supreme hastily remarried, and his second wife had a baby very quickly. None were allowed to see this baby until a year after his birth. The nursemaid of that child is at my estate. She will verify the truth," she answered.

The voices started to become louder. They turned from anger to disgust. Mother held them in the palm of her hand. She took a moment to glance at me and smile. I nodded to her. Now it is my turn.

I waved to Steel. She and a guard walked over to me, carrying a large book and a small table. The guard sat the table down in front of me while Steel laid the book on the table. Their task completed, they returned to the edges of the room. My hands quickly turn to the marked page.

"Here in the elder Supreme's hand, he states that his heir is his second child." I turned to the Supreme. "I must warn you. What I am about to say will hurt you. I know this has been a long family secret, but it must be revealed to save you, Supreme. Your father would not want you to burn for his mistake.”

The Supreme’s face tensed as he slowly nodded.

“Here in his own hand, the late Supreme details the mysterious events that surround his first wife and the protection of his second son from the eyes of his people. The late Supreme stated that he fell in love with his first wife when he was too young. She easily deceived him. Thinking it was true love, he went against all of his advisors and married the penniless woman.”

“That is true,” the eldest councilor stated. “I remember we advised him that it was a mistake to marry someone we knew so little about.”

I nodded solemnly. “How right you were. The late Supreme makes several notes that he had wished he listened to his council. The marriage was wonderful. Their first child was born. But he was not a Normal child. The hands of the child erupted into flames as soon as he was placed in his father’s arms. Soon the truth was revealed. The love of his life was one of the Dragon People. She wasn’t a pureblood. She planned to become a part of the high family of Eurathia, then kill the Supreme, placing her half-breed on the throne. The plan failed when her son bore the marking of their people and the power that they possess."

"And that child is sitting on the throne!" Lady Conrad interrupted, pointing at the Supreme.

I shook my head. "The late Supreme did what he had to do for his kingdom. He had the woman he had thought he loved poisoned. The Supreme couldn't let her vile plans and the taint of her people spread upon this kingdom. Then, he was left with his first child, an innocent. He knew that his firstborn was not at fault. But the blood he held in his veins was too dangerous. He carried the blood of the high family. He was the firstborn—the rightful heir to the throne. The small child's life had to be ended. So with a heavy heart, the late Supreme put to rest the threat to Eurathia. Grief-stricken, the Supreme quickly married, and he had his second son. Paranoid by the threat of the Dragon People, he kept his son safe by preventing anyone from going near him except a select few."

"Are we to believe your word?" Lady Conrad questioned.

"Not my word, but the word of the late Supreme," I answered.

"Of course, he would lie," she continued. "He wouldn't want the kingdom to know that his first and only son is not a pureblood."

"Then perhaps this will prove the late Supreme's words," I said and again waved to Steel.

This time two older women followed. Two chairs were placed in the center of the council. Each woman took a seat. My mother's eyes widened as she saw the lady on the left. She sheepishly returned her gaze.

"This is your evidence, correct, the nursemaid of the current Supreme?" I asked.

Lady Conrad nodded. "How did you take her from the estate?"

"With my will and determination to protect our Supreme," I answered. Then turning to the nursemaid, I asked, "Can you tell the council your name?"

She nodded. "My name is Elise."

"Were you the Supreme's nursemaid throughout his whole childhood?"

"No. I was employed after he was a month old and dismissed when he was four years old," she answered.

"Thank you. Why were you employed after he was a month old?"

"Well, to keep me in the dark of when he was born. I've seen one-month-old babies, Father. He was definitely older," Elise replied.

"If the purpose of hiring you so late was to keep you in the dark, then how did you find out the truth?" I questioned.

"The maid told me," Elise answered.

A burst of muffled laughter startled her.

"It is true," Elise continued. "The maid was the first nursemaid. She snuck back into the castle to make sure the baby was safe. She loved the little one so much."

I pointed to the woman sitting next to her. She wore a scarf over her hair that covered a part of her face. She wore a simple dark gray dress. Elise stood and faced the woman. Her eyes lit up with recognition.

"It is her! Rebecca! It has been so long. I was worried when you disappeared," Elise said, clapping her hands together. Rebecca didn't respond.

"Thank you, Elise," I said and motioned for her to sit down. Then, I turned my attention to Rebecca. "Why would you tell Elise this?"

"It is true," she bit out.

"Is it?" I questioned.

She turned and glared at me. "That child is a half-blood. I was there when he was born."

"You were there, Rebecca, when the first child was born," I said. "Is it true that you cared for the first son?"

"Yes," she answered.

"Is that the little boy you cradled in your arms?" I asked, pointing at the Supreme.

She turned her gaze from me and nodded.

"I don't believe," I stated.

"Why would I lie?" Rebecca shrugged her shoulders.

With one quick movement, I snatched the scarf from her head. The dark red markings of the Dragon People covered her cheeks and her hairline. A loud collective gasp sounded through the council.

"Because, my dear, you are not a Normal. You loved that child because he was one of your own. In fact, the only reason you were employed in the high family's service was that the betrayer, the first wife, had hired you. Your one mission was to take care of that child. But you failed. Didn't you?" I shouted.

Tears formed in her eyes, and her mouth wobbled.

"Tell the truth, Rebecca. You failed that child." I said again in a more sympathetic tone.

She nodded. "I did. That baby didn't get a chance at life. His father murdered him! Murdered that baby because of his bloodline."

"What happened?" I asked.

She dipped her head as the grief shook her shoulders. It took her a long moment before she was able to speak.

"I left with the baby. I thought I would get him to safety, to our people. I didn't know," she paused and placed a hand to her mouth. After another moment, she finished, "I didn't know that his father had poisoned him too. It wasn't long before he died in my arms."

"Then what did you do?" I encouraged.

I buried the sweet child. On his grave, I swore to avenge him."

"How?"

"When I heard that the Supreme had celebrated another child, I was angry. He just replaced that sweet baby as if he never existed. I knew that I wasn't strong enough or capable of killing him. But, I could hurt his legacy."

"His legacy," I prompted.

"I knew Elise. She was just assigned to be the new baby's nursemaid. It was easy to slip back in as a maid. I told her that the baby was the first. It wasn't hard to believe with all the secrets surrounding his birth."

"The lie was born," I said, looking at the council. "This Dragon woman hurt by the death of a baby looked for a way to avenge him. What better way than to have the elder Supreme's line removed from the throne? Have his son be killed by the people he has sworn to lead."

The room became quiet as they stared at Rebecca.

"Mother, for spreading this lie and preparing to betray our Supreme, I place you under arrest. Guards, please take Lady Conrad away."

Three large royal guards flanked my mother. She turned toward me and smiled.

"Well done," she said, then followed the guards out of the room.

"Who else needs to join her?" I asked, facing the council.

Fredrick stood quickly, "I assure you that I had never heard of this evil plot until today."

The balding minion of my mother slowly stood. "I would like to take this moment to apologize to you, Supreme. Lady Conrad had told me of this awful lie. I gave no credit to the situation and believed that she was trying to catch my attention. She was desperate not to let her capable son take control of her estate and lands. I take the blame for allowing her to believe she had support. It is my fault. I took pity on her, for I believed she had lost her sanity. Forgive me. I didn't realize she took it this far."

The Supreme smiled at him. "How can I blame you for your sympathy? I applaud you, good sir. But, I'm afraid that I must strip you of your titles."

The Supreme waved his hand. More royal guards came and

led the flabbergasted councilor out of the room.

"Father Conrad, thank you for restoring my good name. There is now an empty seat in my council. It is yours," the Supreme said.

"Thank you." I bowed. "I am honored to be of service to you."

Checkmate mother. Checkmate.

CHAPTER 2 ARIEL

The crackle of the fire and the smell of the warm broth made my stomach rumble. Jonas handed me a chunk of bread. I picked up a spoon then dipped it into the bubbling broth. I spooned out a bowlful, then sat back down. I took in a deep breath before blowing on the broth. Small chunks of deer meat floated on the surface. My hand dunked the bread into the brown liquid. I feel my lips curve into a smile. I was sitting here eating with my father. Jonas was my father. The happiness that filled my heart was overwhelming. Not only was I free from Conrad's lineage, but I had gained a father in a man that has always been there for me. A man that I have always loved.

"That smells delicious," Michael commented as he entered our campsite.

"Please join us," Freckles said, motioning to an empty spot by the fire.

"Thank you." Michael took a seat.

"Good morning," I said.

Michael smiled at me. "I have some news for all of you. Alex, Jonas, and Ariel, all of you are to sit this mission out. I don't want you anywhere near the Abnormals. Hopefully, before tomorrow, we will conclude our business with them."

"Good," Freckles grinned.

I nodded. "I can do that."

Alex and Jonas agreed.

"That is settled," Michael sighed. "Can I have a bowl of broth?"

Freckles laughed. "Of course," he said, then handed him one.

We all fell into a pleasant conversation about hunting. Apparently, they all enjoyed their last hunt. Even Alex seemed engaged in the conversation. Elizabeth moved closer to me. She leaned against my shoulder as she watched Jonas laugh.

"Michael, we need to talk now!" Edric demanded as he stomped toward us.

I had to suppress a groan. Vivienne joined him. She placed her hands on her hips and glared at me with a fire in her eyes.

"No!" Elizabeth screamed.

I turned to her. "What is wrong?"

She jumped into my arms. I quickly picked her up and held her close. Tears sprung from Elizabeth as her body shook.

"Elizabeth," I said, keeping my voice calm. "Sweetheart, what is wrong."

Freckles rushed over to us. "I will take her to the tent until they leave."

"Thank you," I said as I handed her to him.

Elizabeth snatched the collar of his tunic tightly in her hands. Burying her face into Freckles's chest, Elizabeth's back began to shake with sobs. Mouse followed behind them as Freckles hurried to their tent.

"Why is Elizabeth frightened of you?" I asked, shifting to face them.

Vivienne shrugged. "It is obvious that she is frightened of Winged-People."

I shook my head. "That isn't true. She has never been scared of us."

Vivienne grinned as she looked down at me. "It is because she knows a tool when she sees one."

Alex lunged forward. Jonas placed his hand on his chest. Michael stood and walked to stand in front of them.

"That is enough," Michael said in a low, commanding tone. "You will not insult my friends."

Edric raised his hands. "We meant…"

"Enough!" Michael interrupted. "I'm growing weary of this. What do you want?"

Edric's eyes narrowed as he addressed Michael. "I've heard from Sara that Ariel and her two friends are not coming," he said, pointing at Jonas, then to Alex. "Is this true?"

Michael nodded.

"That is unacceptable," Edric proclaimed.

Vivienne stepped forward, drawing Michael's attention. "How can I leave my son knowing that he is in danger? As soon as Ariel has the chance, she will take him from us."

"She must come on the mission," Edric added.

"This doesn't fit with what we discussed earlier," Michael said. "You told me that you wanted her far away from both of you."

"I know that," Vivienne said. "But as we talked it over, we realized that Ariel would take advantage of our absence."

"Ariel is a part of my team. I will decide how I lead. Now leave," Michael said as he turned his back on them.

"If she stays, Ariel better have guards watching her!" Edric shouted, then turned to leave with Vivienne trailing after him.

Michael let out a long sigh. "They must enjoy causing strife."

"Are we going now?" Jonas laughed.

Michael shook his head. "I believe that all of you should. Edric could be setting Ariel up if she is left behind. It would be easy for them to pretend that she took Seven. But, I won't force anyone to go on this mission. Infiltrating Camp 102 will be dangerous. Everyone that comes knows what they are risking."

"I'm in," Alex announced.

"Me too," I said.

"Count me in as well." Jonas smiled.

Michael nodded.

I excused myself as I went to check on Elizabeth. She laid on a pile of blankets as she cried. Freckles sat next to her rubbing her back while Mouse sat quietly in the corner.

"Did she say what scared her?" I asked.

Freckles shook his head. "Not really. She was repeating fire woman over and over. Something about Vivienne must have brought back that horrible memory. It might have been her hair color."

"I hate to see her like this," I whispered.

Freckles sighed. "What did they even want?"

A bitter laugh escaped my lips. "They were upset that we weren't going on the mission. They seem to think that we will kidnap Seven."

"I really hate them," Freckles seethed.

"Michael thinks they will pretend that we stole Seven if we stay. He is worried that they are setting me up for something. So, he asked us to join the mission," I continued.

"I spoke too soon," Freckles said, shaking his head. "Of course, all of you are going."

I nodded.

"Please be careful. I have a bad feeling about the Abnormals," Freckles warned.

"I do as well. Don't worry. We will be careful."

I reached down and patted Elizabeth on the back. "I will be back soon."

She looked up at me. "Please be careful around the evil woman."

I smiled at her. "I will."

Mouse ran over to me and stretched out her arms. I wrapped her in a tight hug.

"Bye," Mouse said quietly.

"Bye," I said as I released her.

"I will see you tomorrow, little sister," Freckles said.

"Tomorrow." I nodded, then left.

Jonas and Alex had prepped most of the gear we would need. I strapped on my belt and sheath. Jonas handed me my sword, and I quickly sheathed it. Once we were ready, we joined the warriors as they gathered by the remains of last night's bonfire. Simon spotted us in the crowd and waved for us over. We made our way through the packed crowd. He greeted us as soon as we squeezed our way through.

"I heard that plans changed, and all of you are now coming," Simon said.

"That is right," Jonas confirmed. "It was a wonderful display of feigned concern this morning."

"Ah. I'm sorry I missed it." Simon frowned.

"Camp 102 isn't easy to break into. Do you know the plan?" Alex asked.

"Yes, I do. On my last reconnaissance mission, I discovered a portion of the wall had been destroyed. They have yet to start constructing a new section. The guard rotation is a bit slow on the last switch of the night. It should give us enough time to slip in," Simon answered.

Alex crossed his arms. "What about getting out?"

"That will be a little trickier. A small group of us will knock the few guards on duty unconscious as quietly as possible. Then out we will go," Simon said.

"I don't like the last part. There has to be a better way," Alex said.

"That is the only weakness in their defenses. Father Conrad has started to rebuild his forces at this camp. It is a miracle that I found this one." Simon shrugged. "But, I may have a plan to make our escape easier."

"When do we leave?" Jonas asked.

"We will start before noon. It will take us most of the day to reach the Camp. Then, all we do is wait for the shift change."

"How many of our Abnormal friends are joining us?" Jonas smiled.

Simon shook his head. "Not as many as I would've liked."

"Really?" I asked.

Simon nodded. "I believe we have enough for the mission, but a good portion of the warriors remain behind. I had thought they would wait for us close by just in case things go badly."

"That is odd," Jonas stated. "There is more going on here. I wish I could piece it together."

"As do I," Simon added.

CHAPTER 3 CONRAD

It was late in the morning when the Supreme had summoned me to his private study. Dark circles framed his eyes. He stifled a yawn as he greeted me.

"Good morning, Anthony."

"Good morning, Supreme. Did you have a gratifying night?" I asked.

He grinned. "I did. It feels so good to be rid of that horrible woman. I have you to thank for freeing me not only from her but the dark secret that has been haunting me all my life."

"It is my honor," I said.

"You know, I was always afraid that the truth about my lineage would be revealed. It was a horrible dread that ate away at me every day since I learned the truth." The Supreme shook his head. "I am forever in your debt."

"When did you learn the truth?" I asked.

"When my mother or I should say, the woman I believed to be my mother, passed away. My father told me right after the funeral. It was somewhat of a shock," the Supreme said.

"I would imagine," I sympathized.

"That woman, Rebecca, was she my brother's nursemaid?" he asked.

I nodded. "Yes. It took some effort, but my spies were able to find her."

"Was what she said true?" the Supreme looked hesitant. "Did my father really kill my brother?"

"No," I answered. "Rebecca was able to escape with him. She left him in a Dragon village."

A faint smile appeared on the Supreme. "So, my father did have a heart. He said he was dead. I'm actually glad that he is alive. Have you located him?"

"No. If I find your brother, what would you like done?" I asked.

"Bring him to me. I think I would enjoy having a brother." The Supreme laughed. "Now, I have given you a seat on the council, but I feel you deserve more. What can I bestow on you that is worthy of what you have done for me?"

"The only thing that I would ask from you is my mother's life," I answered gravely.

"Are you sure?" He crossed his arms. "She is dangerous."

"I know, but she is my mother. I promise that you will not hear from her again. One toe out of line, and I will end her myself," I declared.

The Supreme nodded. "It is done. Anthony, I feel we have become friends on this day. You know my secret and have protected me from its harm. You could have gained so much if you betrayed me, yet you held firm to your loyalty. You accepted me for who I am. I'm astonished and grateful."

I bowed. "Blood is just blood, Supreme. It is the person that matters. You are my Supreme. You will forever have my loyalty."

The Supreme clapped me on the back. "Be off with you now. I must get my rest. I have an extensive amount of celebrating to-night." He grinned.

I turned and left the Supreme. The only word that rang through my mind was triumph. I had done it. Lady Conrad has been defeated. The Supreme is now beholding to me. Friend. I laughed. He believes we are friends. His weakness is so easy. He longs for acceptance, and now he has found that in me. It will be easy for me to get his approval for what I have planned next. A wicked grin pulled at my lips. I have won, mother. It won't be long now before everything I have longed for will come into being—one piece at a time.

CHAPTER 4 ARIEL

The moon shone between large clouds. Jonas and Alex sat next to me as we waited for the signal. Simon nodded at Michael. The way in was clear. Michael raised his hand. The Rebels crept forward, following him through the gap in Camp 102's wall. The Abnormals stepped into the Camp after us.

"Not many guards stationed around this area," Jonas whispered to Simon.

Simon winked. "That could be attributed to an unofficial reassigning of the guards."

It was dark as we walked to the holding cells. Once we arrived, Tank burned the bars to each cell. Sara and Michael talked to each group. Explaining to them what was happening and encouraging them to stay quiet. The rest of us stood on guard along with the Abnormals. Soon, all of the Blue and Dragon-People were free.

"We must hurry," Simon urged. "It is almost time for the soldiers to return."

As swiftly and quietly as possible, we left the holding cells and made our way back to the gap in the wall. I was amazed by how smoothly this was going. Simon needed to be congratulated for putting all of this into motion.

"Wait." Michael paused and looked around us. "Where are the Abnormals?"

"What happened to them?" Simon wondered.

"Sara, take charge of our forces and lead the survivors out of the camp. Wait for me by the river," Michael ordered.

Sara nodded, then motioned for the rest of the Rebels to follow her.

"Well, we are not leaving you behind," Tank said, crossing his arms.

"Shall we go investigate what is keeping our partners?" Sy asked.

Michael nodded.

Alex, Jonas, and I joined them as we retraced our steps back to the holding cells. Shouts and sounds of battle could be heard as we approached. Drawing our weapons, we quickly entered the battle. Normals had amassed a medium-sized force. The soldiers rained down on the Abnormals. Edric's laughter could be heard over the battle. Michael fought his way over to him. I followed.

"What happened?" Michael asked in between strikes of his sword.

More laughter from Edric, and then he answered. "My dear friend," he chuckled. "Did you actually think we would leave this place without killing every single Normal in it?"

My mouth dropped. Michael tensed. It was them. All this time, it was them.

"You," Michael said. "You were the ones burning the villages?"

Edric nodded. "And slaughtering every single Normal living there."

Michael lowered his sword. "We won't be a part of this."

Edric turned to him. "You have no choice now. They won't let you leave. They will track you to your precious Rebels and all of the innocents you protect. You have to join me in the slaughter tonight." Edric laughed again wildly.

A low growl emitted from Michael. "You will pay for what you have done!"

"Perhaps, my friend but not today," Edric countered.

"Fight your way out!" Michael shouted to us.

We moved through the crowd as more Normals swarmed into the fray. Soon, we had no choice but to stand our ground and fight. More soldiers now blocked the path out. We formed our circle—each of us protecting the others' back. Tank would shoot a burst of flame, then Sy and Jonas would strike. Alex and I took turns fighting off the Normals between Michael's blasts of energy. This continued for what seemed like the whole night. Sweat poured off my shoulders, and I pushed myself to fight on. My muscles seemed to bleed out strength with each blow I struck. Tank shot out another large flame, then our last opponents fell. No one else ran to take their place. I looked over at the Abnormals. Shouts of victory sounded from them as they celebrated.

Rage darkened Michael's face as he marched over to Edric. The rest of us followed, sharing in his anger. Edric turned to face Michael with a broad smile on his face.

"You would make an excellent addition to our team even if you are Blue," Edric laughed.

Without warning, Michael slammed his fist right into Edric's face. He fell to his knees. Michael gazed down at him with all the fury burning inside of him.

"You tricked our team into helping you murder these people. It was never about saving the Freaks in the holding cells," Michael thundered.

"What does it matter?" Edric argued. "We both got what we wanted."

"It matters to me!" Michael's voice boomed.

"What do you care about these Normals? They are nothing but a plague to our kind. Isn't it better that we wipe them out?" Edric shrugged.

"They are living beings. People! You can't wipe out a race of people. You can't go in with intentions to murder everyone. That makes us no better than what we are fighting against," Michael voiced.

"The only thing I am fighting for is their extinction. And as I see it, you are either with us or against us. Are these people worth your effort to save?" Edric reasoned. "Are they worth a war with us?" Edric stood up and looked Michael in the eyes. "Do you think your people could handle a war with mine?"

"We will never stand with you!" Michael raged.

"Then so be it. War is what you will get. I hope you are ready. I hope the people back at your camp are ready?" Edric laughed.

"Back to camp!" Vivienne yelled. "Let's make these fools see the mistake in refusing us!"

The Abnormals took to the sky. Disbelief flooded through me. They wouldn't attack all of the innocent people at camp, would they? A sick feeling rose up in my throat. Of course, they would. They have murdered innocent villagers. Children. No one is safe from their cruelty. Michael's eyes shone a dark blue as he raised his hand into the air. The wind from his power swooshed past me. A blue shield appeared above the Abnormals. A yell escaped Michael's lips as he lowered his hand, causing the shield to drop.

Shocked cries could be heard from the Abnormals as they fell from the sky beyond the wall.

"I don't know how long that will delay them," Michael said, breathing hard.

Without another word, we raced out of the camp and headed toward the river. There wasn't a moment to waste. The Abnormals had declared war on us. They were nothing but brutal animals. They would hurt and kill anyone. Freckles, Elizabeth, and Mouse would be at their mercy. What mercy? They wouldn't hesitate to murder them and every innocent man, woman, and child there. Please, Please, let us stop them. Please let us get there in time to save everyone.

CHAPTER 5 ARIEL

Early morning light shone down on the devastation that was left of the camp. A few Abnormals were filling their arms with food from barrels. Spreading out my wings, I threw myself into the air hurtling toward them. Startled, some of them began to run. One raised their arms as I slashed my sword through their skin. A cry of pain sounded from him as he collapsed to the ground. Sy and Tank ran past me as they chased down the others.

My feet shifted, and I ran with all my might to our tents. I froze when I saw Freckles lying face down on the ground.

"No!" I screamed as I raced toward him. "Freckles!"

He slowly shifted to his side. "Ariel."

Alex and Jonas were on my heels. Jonas slid to the ground. He ripped the edges of his tunic as he applied pressure to the deep wound on Freckles' shoulder.

"Vivienne," Freckles mumbled. "after….she was after the girls. The woods." Freckles nodded with his head in the direction Vivienne had gone.

Panic rushed through me as I bolted into the trees.

"I'm with you," Alex said as he ran next to me.

Swords in hand, we ran. There in the distance, I could see the girls huddled together. I pushed my feet into an even faster pace. They jumped as Alex and I appeared before them. Elizabeth had a trail of blood running down her face as Mouse clung to her. I sank to my knees in front of them and wrapped my arm around both of them. Their bodies trembled with their tears. I patted their backs and calmed them down.

"You are okay," I said. "We are here."

Elizabeth pulled back and looked at me. "She tried to kill us."

"What happened?" I asked.

"Vivienne is the same woman that attacked me before,"

Elizabeth cried. "She hurt Freckles. He fought with her, but he didn't have a weapon. He yelled at us to run. I grabbed Mouse and hid here." Elizabeth stopped and grabbed her face. Sobs shook her shoulders. "Freckles. Where is Freckles?"

"Jonas is with him," I answered. "He is alive."

"Vivienne told me that she had to finish what she started. That I was going to die today, and she would give my body to you as a gift." Elizabeth's voice trembled.

I squeezed her shoulder. "I'm so sorry."

"That vile woman! I want to strangle her!" Alex shouted, then took a deep breath. "How did you escape her?"

"Seven and Red saved us," Elizabeth answered. "They told her they spotted the Rebels coming. They needed to leave. And she did."

I pulled Elizabeth back into my arms and held her tightly. "You and Mouse are safe now. Vivienne will never hurt you again. I promise."

"We need to end this," Alex declared. "We get Seven and Red out. Then, we finish the Abnormals."

I nodded. "The Abnormals want a war; then we will give them

a war."

CHAPTER 6 ARIEL

My hand rested on Freckles' arm as I informed Michael and him what Elizabeth told me. Michael wore a deep frown while Freckles listened solemnly. My thoughts kept returning to Seven.

"Michael," I began. "I have to go after them. I need to rescue Seven and Red. The Abnormals need to pay for what they did." I said as my fingers squeezed Freckle's arm.

Freckles laid his hand on top of mine. "That is not what I want. What I want is for you to stop fighting."

I sighed. "I can't let them continue. They must be stopped. Not to mention that Seven and Red are trapped."

"I agree," Michael said. "They must be stopped. Now is not the time. We have doubled the number of survivors in our group. We must take them to the fort. At this rate, we may not make it to Blue Land until spring. We may have to spend winter at the fort. I want these people out of danger and starting their new lives as soon as possible."

"Leave Seven and Red?" I questioned.

"No. For now, Seven is safe. Red will take care of him. These people will not survive if we wait too much longer. The patrols have increased because of the Abnormals. We have to be smart. Once we get the survivors to the fort, we can plan how to save Seven and Red and how to deal with the Abnormals. There will be more warriors at the fort. We could divide our forces. One group of warriors to escort the survivors to the Blue territory, and the other half will come with us."

I sighed. "I don't know if I can wait."

Michael took in a deep breath, then looked down before he responded. "Ariel, believe me when I say I understand. There is nothing I want more than to rush into this mission. But, we have to strategize carefully. As we sit now, we wouldn't stand a chance against them. Wounded and exhausted from the last battle and the journey. If we leave to hunt them, we risk the survivors. They could be discovered. We could be killed, and the survivors would be left defenseless. Or we would have to journey through winter to the fort."

"Michael," I said, shaking my head.

"Please trust me," he said. "I promise you that we will deal with the Abnormals and bring Seven and Red home with us."

I ran my hand over my head. My heart wanted me to refuse, but deep down, I knew this was the right choice.

"I trust you, Michael."

"Thank you," he said, then turned to Freckles. "I wish we could wait here for everyone to recover, but we must move."

Freckles nodded. "I will be alright."

Michael patted his shoulder then stood up. "Make ready to move. We will leave as soon as everyone is loaded. I will have a wagon prepared to make room for Freckles and the girls. It will come to pick them up."

"Thank you," I said, then Michael left.

"You rest," I ordered Freckles. "I will help the others pack."

It took us a long time to pack. Jonas and I sorted through the items, packing the things not too damaged. It was hard to see the tent and blankets that we had called home the past few weeks turned to bits and pieces of charred material. The crunching of wheels on dried leaves drew my attention. Alex drove a wagon up to us. It was already full of injured Dragon-People.

"I guess I'm on wagon duty," Alex commented as I walked over to him. "Too many were injured, and now we are short on drivers."

I smiled at him. "That was nice of you to help."

Alex shrugged.

"I will get the Freckles and the girls," I said.

Freckles stood up off the blankets while Jonas quickly folded them. The bandage around Freckles' shoulder was clean as I surveyed it.

"Alex is ready with the wagon," I said.

Freckles nodded. Elizabeth and Mouse helped Jonas with blankets. I picked up two large packs. That was all that remained from our camp. Jonas picked up Elizabeth, then Mouse, and sat them into the wagon. Freckles climbed in, waving off Jonas's help. I sat the packs in the back.

"We are all loaded," Jonas called to Alex.

Alex nodded. "See you soon."

Alex moved off to join the line of wagons beginning to form. Jonas and I followed. We walked silently. We weren't the only ones. It was unusual how quiet everyone was. It was typical for laughter and loud voices to echo through the forest as we gathered to start a day's journey. But, there was nothing but silence as we prepared. Everyone was reflecting on yesterday's events, the wounded, and the brave souls lost.

"Ariel," a voice called my name. I turned around, surprised to see Isaac. He limped heavily on a crunch. His right leg was wrapped in a bandage from his knee down.

"What happened?" I asked.

"It is nothing," Isaac said. "I will recover."

"I'm glad. It has been too long since we last talked." I said. "Would you like to walk with us?"

Isaac shook his head. "No. I prefer to be alone. I wanted to tell you that I'm sorry about Seven. And if you need anything, please ask."

"Thank you," I said.

Isaac nodded, then hurried away from me. Jonas squeezed my shoulder.

"Don't take it personally," Jonas whispered. "He is suffering."

"I hate to see him this way." I sighed.

"I know. Give Isaac time and patience. He will come around," Jonas said.

My fingers squeezed Jonas's hand. "Thank you, father."

A slight blush crept over Jonas's cheeks. "You're welcome, daughter."

CHAPTER 7 ARIEL

It took two days to reach the fort inside of Blue Territory. We left the protection of the woods as we entered the structure constructed with stone. Giant Mountains framed the fort. As we passed the gate, we were met with a large force of Rebels. Michael and Sara were greeted by what seemed to be the leader. Jonas patted my arm, then walked over to Simon. They began talking almost immediately. I smiled. It was so good to see him happy. Alex jumped down from the wagon and stretched.

"My body is killing me from bouncing in that wagon the whole way here," he groaned.

"I agree," Freckles said as he climbed down.

Elizabeth and Mouse followed, each of them stretching. I took a moment to study this Blue fort. It had an open field in the middle. All of the buildings were placed against the wall. A few small wooden buildings were in front of one large metal structure that must hold supplies. Nothing seemed extravagant. There was a place with a small garden, but it hadn't been well maintained.

"Is this our new home?" Mouse asked.

"No," I answered. "We are just stopping here before we make the final part of our journey."

"We aren't going to leave Seven?" Mouse looked up at me with wide eyes.

I smiled as I knelt beside her. "Of course, we're not. I will bring him back."

"Good," she grinned. "I miss Seven."

"We all do," Freckles said.

A loud cry echoed through the fort. I froze.

"What was that?" Elizabeth whispered.

Soon smoke filled the air. Alex and I glanced at each other. Panic in both of our eyes. The gates are still open! Alex sprinted toward them. I spun around toward Freckles and directed him to get the wagon out of the open.

"We are under attack!" A Rebel shouted.

The sky darkened as it was filled with the Abnormals. My heart fell. I picked up Elizabeth, then Mouse, and placed them in the wagon.

"Go!" I yelled at Freckles.

He slapped the reins, urging the horses into a gallop. The wagon lurched away from me. The Abnormals attacked from the sky and flooded in through the gate. How many of them were there? I unsheathed my sword and shifted into a battle stance. In a matter of moments, I was rushed by several Winged-People. The clash of metal against metal rang out with the cries of the wounded. Smoke burned through the air. The Abnormals set fire to anything that would ignite.

It was an endless stream of Freaks. A warrior swung a heavy ax toward my head. My knees crashed onto the ground. The wind of the blade brushed the back of my neck. I rolled away, then kicked the warrior in the knees with all the force I could muster. His knee snapped backward. The warrior let out a cry as he fell beside me. I finished him. A hand gripped the back of my tunic and pushed me onto my stomach. I scrambled to my feet. In front of me stood a giant Winged-man. He was bald, with scars all over his body. He grinned at me. The act sent a shiver down my spine. He spread out his brown wings and bolted to me. I jumped into the air and flipped over him, landing on my feet. He yelled as he turned around. He drew a large sword that took both of his hands to hold. The sword crashed into mine. I gritted my teeth as I forced my sword to block. Again he swung. This time his sword snapped my blade in half. My fingers released the useless weapon. He laughed as he stared down at me, then he lunged.

My fingers curled into a fist, then slammed hard into his face. Blood squirted out of it as his nose made a loud crunch sound. The punch didn't slow him down, as the giant returned the punch, dropping his sword. Another crunch sound echoed in my ears, but this time it was my own nose. Blood ran down my face. I placed my hands on his shoulders and brought both of my knees up into his stomach. He gasped for air and fell to the ground. Blood filled my mouth. I spat onto the dirt and wiped the blood away from my face before turning back toward him. He nodded at me.

"Not bad," he chuckled. "Not good enough, though."

He charged. My feet kicked the ground as I climbed into the air. I had to get some momentum on the next hit. I groaned as his fingers wrapped around my ankle. He jerked me down, and I slammed onto the ground—air leaving my body. I coughed as I rolled on my side.

A pain imploded inside of my stomach as his large foot connected. A cry escaped my lips as another kick hit my chest. Again and Again, the kicks kept coming. I was defenseless. My mind couldn't think of how to get out of this. Finally, they stopped. I glanced up to see not just the giant but Edric as well.

"Take her," Edric ordered.

The giant grinned down at me as he slammed his boot into my

face. Then, there was nothing but darkness.

CHAPTER 8 CONRAD

Dark clouds hung in the sky as the cold breeze forced me to tighten my coat. The carriage pulled to a stop in front of a large cottage. Servants were bustling about preparing it to be lived in. I slowed my horse and stopped next to the carriage. The door swung open, and my mother stepped down. She huddled deeper into her furs.

Lady Conrad narrowed her eyes once she caught sight of me. "Is this to be my cell?"

I smiled. "Think of it as your new home. Your every need will be taken care of as long as you choose to live a quiet life. But your life will be over in an instant if there is even a hint of trouble from you. Mother, you have many years left. Live them peacefully."

She sniffed. "I want my servant returned."

"Steel," I said. "Would you fetch my mother's servant?"

Steel nodded, then rode off to the supply wagon, slowly making its way up the grassy hill.

"You think I can be content here?" She asked.

"I hope," I answered. "I hope you will."

Steel returned with a large box sitting in her lap. She dismounted her horse and then set the box at my mother's feet. Lady Conrad's hands trembled as she removed the lid. Inside was the rotten head of her servant. His mouth hung open in a death cry. The smell quickly infected the air. Lady Conrad straightened quickly. Her face was red with rage. Shock pulsed through me as I noticed a tear that fell down her face. How surprising! She cared for him.

"You!" Lady Conrad shouted. "You may have won this battle, but not the war. Not the war! I will crush you!"

My body slid down the horse and approached her. "Mother, it is over. You have lost the power you had. The Conrad lands are now mine. This cottage and peaceful life I offer you is a mercy—the last I will ever give you. Mother, you tore out my heart with what you did to my family. Without even a thought for my happiness, you destroyed my whole world. Take this life. Perhaps you will grow to love it. This quiet life was all I ever wanted."

"I do not fear you!" She replied. Her body shook with all of her anger. "You lack the strength to kill me, or you would have already done it at the council meeting."

I shook my head and laughed lightly. "The remaining feeling I have for you is in this mercy. Never doubt my ability to kill. It is because of you that I can turn myself into a monster. That wonderful school you sent me to and the rehabilitation center you put me through twice has honed that ability to transform myself into an unfeeling murdering monster." I leaned closer to her and lowered my voice. "One toe out of line, you will get to meet your creation, mother."

With that, I turned and mounted my horse. "Let's go, Steel. Mother, the servants will help you get settled. I apologize that I can't stay longer and show you around your new home. Perhaps on another visit, we can spend more quality mother and son time together."

She glared at me. The ice in her eyes completely melted and all that remained was pure hatred for me.

"Goodbye, mother."

Steel and I left, heading back to the mansion. I was anxious to get back to work and start building my dream.

"Congratulations, Father. You won," Steel said.

I grinned. "This part is done. However, there is still plenty more work to be done before we are finished. But, I do believe that we can at least celebrate this milestone. Lady Conrad's reign is over. Now, it is my chance to build a legacy that will change Eurathia."

"Father, this letter came for you," Steel said. "The messenger said it was urgent that you got this."

Steel reached out toward me. I took the note from her and studied the parcel. The seal was in the shape of a crow. I frowned. My fingers tightened as I pulled the letter free from the wax. The letter was long. Taking a moment to quickly scan it, surprise ran through me.

"This is interesting," I mused aloud.

"What is it?" Steel asked.

"It is a letter from an organization I have never heard of. They call themselves the Order of the Crows, and they want my help," I answered.

"With what?" Steel questioned.

"That is the interesting part," I said. "They didn't say."

Steel frowned.

"But, we will find out. They want to meet us back at the capital. Care for a little detour?" I smiled.

Steel nodded. "I'm curious, Father. You don't think it is a trap."

I shrugged. "Perhaps it is. Perhaps it isn't. But, the Order of the Crows has caught my attention. Another piece has been added to the board, Steel. And we must uncover if that piece is an alley or a foe."

CHAPTER 9 JONAS

I sucked in deep breaths as I watched the Abnormals retreat. My hands ripped out my daggers from one of the attackers. He lay lifeless in the dirt. Fools. They had to force this hatred. We have done nothing to them. They have lost their minds for their need to destroy.

A few of the survivors cried while they told Sara about a missing family member. I slowly made my way to Freckles. More people were searching and calling loudly for friends that were missing. Michael waved me over.

"Are you alright?" I asked as I walked over to him.

He nodded. "You?"

"Fine. Just a few cuts, but they will heal," I answered.

"Have you seen Ariel?" Michael frowned as he surveyed the fort. "I haven't been able to find her. She wasn't with Freckles."

"No," I answered, fighting down the panic. "I will tell Ariel that you are looking for her."

"Thank you." Michael smiled.

I continued toward the gate. Alex leaned heavily against the wall.

"Alex," I called.

He nodded.

"Where is Ariel?" I shouted.

He turned his head, looking behind me. He squinted, then looked in a different direction. He straightened, then rushed over to me.

"She is not where I last saw her," he said.

I swallowed down my nerves. "We just had a battle. Of course, she won't be in the same spot. Help me look for her."

Alex nodded, then we looked. And we looked. Time seemed to speed past us as we searched every part of the fort. Soon we enlisted the help of Sy and Tank but to no avail. We couldn't find her. Sara said that she would check the dead. My heart froze at her words. Again, Alex and I frantically searched. It wasn't until we reached the stables that Sara had found us.

"Finally, I found both of you," Sara said.

"No," Alex said. He raised both of his hands. "Please don't tell me. She is not with the dead." His voice cracked as he turned from us. "She can't be," he blurted, his voice going hoarse.

Sara walked over to Alex and gently placed her hand on his shoulder. My breath caught in my throat. Everything seemed to slow down. My heart pounded in my ears. She looked at me, then Alex.

"She is not there," Sara whispered.

Alex's shoulders shook as he turned his head away.

"Where is she?" I asked.

"The Abnormals have kidnapped several of the survivors as well as some of our warriors. Michael and I believe that Ariel was among the ones taken," Sara stated. "She is alive."

"Then what are we waiting for? Let's go after them," Alex urged.

"Come with me," Sara said. "Michael is coming up with a plan."

We followed Sara across the fort to where Michael leaned over a large table. He was staring intently at a map. The wind blew wildly, making the edges of the heavy paper dance. Michael's face was unreadable. It wasn't until our shadows covered the map did he raise his head.

"You know?" He asked.

I nodded.

"Those fiends! It will take us about two days to prepare. First, we have to get the survivors on their trek to the new settlement. Then, the forces must be divided. It will take time."

"Two days!" Alex shouted. "You want to wait two days while Ariel is at the Abnormals' mercy. Edric and Vivienne will kill her. We can't wait two days. Now! We leave now!"

Michael sighed. "That would be foolish. We need to get the survivors moving. We need to prepare our forces so we can stop the Abnormals. We will be attacking them at their camp. They will have the advantage. None of us knows how many of them there are. We must prepare well if we want to save Ariel."

"You are serious! Wait! You can sit here and stare at your map. Jonas, let's go," Alex said, turning to leave.

"Stop!" Michael commanded. "You will get yourselves killed. How will that help? Not only will you both die, but your presence will warn the Abnormals of our attack. How will any of this help Ariel?"

"Waiting is putting her life at risk. Every moment she is with them, Ariel moves closer to being killed. Or worse, they could be torturing her." Alex started pacing back and forth. "How can you just sit there?"

Michael sighed. "I care for her just as much as you do."

"Liar!" Alex yelled. "If you did, you wouldn't be sitting there calm."

Michael slammed his fist onto the table, releasing the map and letting it fly off. "Calm! You think I am calm! Every inch of me wants to race out there! But I'm not an idiot!"

Alex stepped forward. "Idiot? And giving Edric and Vivienne the chance to torture her to death is the smart choice!"

Both men stood face to face with their bodies tense. A fight was about to erupt between them. I pushed myself in the middle.

"Enough!" I said. "Ariel and every single one of our people needs our help. Fighting amongst ourselves gets us nowhere and gives the Abnormals more time to inflict pain on our loved ones.

Everyone is counting on us to save them, right now. The three of us know what invading their camp will be like. It will be a war. Alex, do you go to war with unprepared troops?"

Alex glared down at me.

"Do you?" I demanded.

He sighed. "No."

"Michael, is two days the best we can do? Can we afford to wait two days?"

Michael shook his head.

"Good. We have agreed. This is what we do. Sara will organize and get the survivors out of here. She will take a third of the warriors while the rest will go with us. The three of us will prepare them. Dawn is when we will leave. Agreed?"

Alex and Michael nodded in agreement.

"Good. Now, let's get to work," I ordered.

CHAPTER 10 ARIEL

My back hit against something hard. A pounding in my head increased as I slowly opened my eyes. My hands were bound together along with my wings. My face was shoved into someone's back. I shifted around as best I could. My eyes stung by the brightness of the sun overhead. The wagon bounced furiously as trees sped past us. I raised both my hands to my face. Blood had dried over my nose and cheeks. My fingers lightly touched my nose. It came to life with pain.

"Are you okay," I whispered to the man next to me.

Silence was my only response. I tried again. Still, he didn't answer. One of the Abnormals rode up to the wagon and glared down at me. She pulled a whip off her belt and swung it down on my chest. Crack! The whip slapped against the man and me. A cry of pain came from him. I gritted my teeth, letting the rage fuel me through the sting.

"Quiet!" She hissed at us.

The wagon continued its bumpy trek until the trees thinned out, and the sound of running water echoed around us. The Abnormals halted, then disappeared. The noise of greeting their companions and laughter was all we heard. The sun rose even higher in the sky. A cold wind rushed over the top of the wagon. The Abnormals took their time before dealing with us. Edric's voice boomed, ordering a group to help him with the prisoners. I braced myself as the back of the wagon opened. Edric grinned as our eyes met. He reached for my feet and pulled me out. The edge of the wagon rushed up toward me. Without my hands to catch or brace myself, I fell on my wings against the hard, uneven ground. More laughter came from them as they continued their amusement of dragging us by our feet.

Edric and his minions took us to an area that had a small campfire. They placed all of the Rebels around the fire. Edric bent down over me.

"You get to have a special place to stay while with us, Ariel." He chuckled.

Edric grabbed my feet and dragged me to a large campfire surrounded by several tents. Laughter followed me. Once Edric released my feet, a rock hit me on my stomach. More rocks followed. I rolled to my side, covering my face. My wings tried to stretch out, but the ropes held them in place.

"Stop it! Stop it!" I heard Seven's voice scream.

Soon small hands wrapped around my head, and the rocks immediately stopped. Voices yelled at Seven to move. Seven refused. The demands grew louder, but Seven's feet didn't budge.

"Edric," a female voice complained. "What is wrong with your son? Can we just hit him with the rocks too?"

Panic rushed through me. "Seven," I yelled. "Move. Seven, move away!"

"I'm not going to leave you," Seven declared.

"Are you really asking to hurt one of our own?" A surge of relief flooded me as I heard Red's voice.

"Edric, is this what the Abnormals are about?" Red asked.

"No," Edric said. "Enough fun, my friends. Don't worry. There will be plenty more opportunities. Go get some food and rest."

Footsteps stomped over to us, and Seven was pulled away from me. He tripped and fell. Edric bent down and stared at Seven with anger twisting his face.

"Don't you ever humiliate me again. She is an enemy. Torture and death are the fate of all who oppose us. You need to become strong, Nathaniel. Or your fate will be just like Ariel's." Edric warned, then stood.

"You are disgusting!" I shouted at him. "You threaten your son!"

Edric turned to me and smiled wickedly. "There is nothing you can do about it, Camp Freak. Worry more about yourself. Death is coming, and it won't be quick."

He straightened, then walked off. Seven rushed into the tent. Within a few minutes, he returned with a wet cloth. Seven gently began washing the blood and dirt from me. Tears dripped down his face. I didn't know what to tell him. How do I prepare someone to watch a loved one be tortured and killed?

"Seven, I will finish up. You better head inside," Red said.

"Okay," Seven said, his voice sounding so small.

Seven handed him the dirty cloth, then walked away. Red helped me sit up. He grimaced when he saw my face.

"Do I look that bad?" I said, trying to smile.

"Worse," Red grinned.

"Can you do me a favor?" I asked.

Red nodded.

"Please watch over Seven for me. And…if you can spare him from watching what happens to me."

"Of course," Red said. "They are insane. All of them are bloodthirsty animals." Red leaned in close, then whispered. "Michael gave me this mission in secret. I never really wanted to join them. My whole purpose was to learn more about them and protect Seven. I will get Seven away from them. He will grow up in the Blue Territory. I promise you." Red took a deep breath. "I promise you. He will be free. Your dream will come true."

"Thank you," I said, my voice cracking with emotion.

Red stood quickly and hid the cloth behind his back. Vivienne frowned as she approached us. She placed a slender hand on her hip, then sighed.

"Red, I worry about you." Vivienne shook her head. "Being seen with the enemy will make it difficult for you to become one of us. You do want to become an Abnormal?"

"Yes," Red answered. "I want to make the Normals pay for what they did to me."

Vivienne smiled slightly. "Good. Now run along. I need to have a chat with our guest."

Red nodded, then walked away. I didn't look at him as he left. That would only put him in more danger than he already was. I must distance myself as much as possible from Red during my last days. Please let me be strong enough to endure their torture.

"My sweet little Camp Freak, how are you enjoying your stay at our home?" She laughed. "I wonder how you would have reacted if you joined us freely? Your compassion for the Normals would fall on deaf ears here. Your naïve morals would have gotten in your way of truly living a full life." Vivienne sat next to me and patted the top of my head. "Poor child," she cooed. "It must be difficult being an abomination. Neither Freak nor Normal wants to claim you." She ran a finger down the scar on my face. "You are fighting for the very people who scarred you." A bitter laugh erupted from her. "Pathetic."

Vivienne pulled a small stick from the fire. The end had a small flame burning the wood. She brought it up to my arm. I could feel the heat of the fire against my skin.

"One of my favorite things is fire. It burns everything. It doesn't matter if you are a Winged-Freak, Normal, or even an abomination like you." The firelight danced across her face as a wicked grin appeared. "Fire is so pretty to watch. Its touch leaves a permanent mark on your body and soul. Here, feel."

Vivienne pressed the flame on my arm. Pain shot through me. My teeth sank into my lips as I refused to scream. Burning of flesh filled my nostrils. Laughter bubbled from her. Water filled my eyes as the intensity grew. Then she sat the stick back into the campfire. My arm throbbed.

"Now, you will have a reminder of me," Vivienne whispered, then stood. "We will have so much fun killing you and the rest of your friends. My fire will consume all of the Rebels and every Normal. One by one, they will all burn."

CHAPTER 11 JONAS

Simon waved to Sara as she led the survivors to the settlement in the Blue Territory. An ax hit the ground with a loud thud. I glanced to my right to see Freckles practicing with the weapon. He struggled with his injured arm.

"Where are the girls?" I questioned.

"Isaac is coming around with a wagon for them. They are waiting near the gate." Freckles pointed.

I followed him back to the fort. The girls sat patiently for him. Mouse looked up at him with worry in her eyes.

"Are you not going with them?" I asked.

Freckles shook his head. "I'm not going to sit this one out." He looked at me. "I know I'm not a warrior, but she is my sister. I'm not going to leave her behind while I go to…." Freckles lowered his head, unable to finish.

"You are not leaving her behind," I said. "Ariel wouldn't want you to leave the girls."

"She is in so much trouble," Freckles whispered.

"I know. But, we will save her. You need to take these girls to safety and pick us out a great spot to live. That way, when we return, Ariel will have a home," I reasoned. "Don't do this. Ariel would want you to protect Mouse and Elizabeth. Besides, Freckles your arm. How effective do you think you will be with that arm? You can barely raise it. I don't want to be mean, but Freckles, you will get yourself killed. Then, how will that help Ariel? How will that help Mouse and Elizabeth? These girls need you. Ariel knows that."

Freckles sighed. "You're right. I'm being foolish. When we see each other again, I will have our house ready."

Isaac and Alex rode up on the wagon. They had filled it full of supplies. Alex hopped off and stood next to me. Mouse ran over to us. She gave Alex and then me a hug. Alex picked her up and placed her in the wagon. Elizabeth walked over and hugged me. Then she walked up to Alex. He bent down on his knees. She took a deep breath.

"Be careful," she said.

Alex nodded.

"Bring back Ariel and Seven," Elizabeth said, tears forming in her eyes.

"I will," Alex said.

"Alex," Elizabeth whispered. "Please make sure Vivienne never hurts us again. I have already lost one family to her. I can't lose another. Please stop her."

Alex wrapped his arms around her. "I promise."

Elizabeth kissed him on the cheek. Alex leaned back, surprise on his face. Elizabeth smiled at him before running to Freckles.

Alex stared at her with disbelief. I grinned. Alex has endured so much growing up. He has never been loved or accepted for who he is. Elizabeth may not realize what she did, but she just cut through the years of rejection and made him feel wanted. Alex was accepted by a girl that has every reason to fear and hate Winged-People. Alex glanced at me, then stood trying to hide his emotions.

"See you soon," Elizabeth called out to us as she climbed up on the wagon.

I waved at her. Alex gave her a smile, a real smile. Children have a way of seeing through the masks we keep to hide ourselves. Elizabeth saw through Alex's. His uncaring and rough appearances are a mask he keeps to protect his fragile heart. It is no different than how Ariel accepted me after I had returned from my re-education. Ariel had every reason to hate Normals, but she saw through my mask just as Elizabeth sees through Alex's.

Isaac frowned at Freckles as he sat next to him in the wagon. "I thought you were going?"

Freckles shook his head. "I had some sense talked into me." Freckles faced us. "A home will be there when you return with Ariel and Seven."

"Safe travels, Freckles," I waved.

Isaac waved. "Good luck," he said, then the wagon jumped forward as they rushed to catch up with the group.

Simon walked over to us and sighed. "Are you ready?"

I nodded.

"When do we leave?" Alex asked.

"The men are just finishing loading supplies. We will be leaving shortly," Simon answered.

The three of us walked through the gate. The horses stood in the center. The riders checked their saddles. Michael walked next to Tank and Sy as he rolled up a map. There are roughly 50 warriors here ready to save our kidnapped loved ones and end the Abnormals. This would be a battle unlike any I have faced. To fight a force of Winged-People was a new experience.

Their technique was so unlike how the elite were trained. The Abnormals used their wings and flight consistently throughout their battles. Our elites used flight and wings as a surprise tactic. We will need every drop of battle experience and warriors to face the Abnormals head-on. I hope our invasion of their camp will catch them off guard enough to seal our victory.

Fear gnawed at my heart. What if we were too late? How long will the Abnormals torture Ariel before they get bored and kill her? I sucked in a deep breath. How long can Ariel survive their brutalities?

Simon squeezed my shoulder. "We will save them."

I nodded. "I hope we do."

"Ariel is strong. She isn't alone. Red and Seven are there. And if there is one thing I know about Ariel," Simon said with a small laugh. "When Seven is in trouble, Ariel can defy the impossible. Believe me, my friend. We will save them."

CHAPTER 12 JONAS

The wind tugged on our clothes as we marched forward. Simon scouted ahead. We all hoped that the Abnormals' base wasn't too far. The day was quickly turning to night. Soon, we would have to stop. It would do us no good to charge into battle tired. Though, I don't know how much sleep any of us will get.

Alex had remained silent the entire trek. Every attempt I made at a conversation ended before it even started. My heart ached for Ariel. Alex must be feeling the same pain. We needed a task. I'm sure Simon could use a break.

"Let's give Simon a hand," I suggested to Alex.

He nodded.

We urged our horses into a gallop and headed toward Simon. He was a good distance away. It would take us some time to catch up. I nodded to Michael and Tank as we passed them.

"Going to help Simon," I called back to them.

"Tell Simon to keep going. We won't be stopping," Michael yelled.

My hands pulled the reins, then turned the horse around. Alex followed. I rode up next to Michael.

"We aren't going to stop?" I asked. "Is that wise?"

Michael shrugged. "Probably not. My patience is wearing thin. I want to be there. Too much time has passed. If we continue, it will cut our travel in half. Perhaps, we will take turns sleeping in the wagons. I don't want to stop."

Tank sighed. "She will be okay, Michael. We have to believe that she will be okay."

Michael swallowed hard.

"I will let Simon know," I said. "I will relieve him. Simon will need some rest."

"Tank, prepare the wagons," Michael ordered.

"Of course," Tank said. "I believe we can fit close to five people at a time."

"Good," Michael said.

Tank turned his horse around and left to carry out his orders. I nodded to Michael, then Alex and I quickened our horses to a faster pace. It wasn't long before we were alone. The silence between Alex and I grew heavy. Alex stretched out his wings, then rolled his neck. I could feel his worry.

"Make sure you get some rest," I said.

"I won't sleep until Ariel is safe," Alex stated.

"You will be no good to her if you're too exhausted to fight," I reasoned.

"How can I sleep when she is afraid? Right now, Ariel could be hurting from their torture. Sleep! How can I possibly rest?" Alex's voice faded to a whisper. "When she could be dead."

I sucked in a deep breath. Dead. That word. That horrible word. My heart clenched. Slowly, I breathed in, willing my heart to calm.

"Alex, you can't think that way," I said.

"You don't understand. Ariel…Ariel is special to me," Alex voiced.

"And she is not to me?" I laughed.

He groaned. "That isn't what I meant."

"Tell me, Alex. It will make you feel better. Believe it or not, I was in love once."

His eyes shot to mine. "I didn't say love."

I raised my eyebrow. "You didn't need to."

"Love," Alex whispered. "I do love her. My heart yearns for her. It hurts; it physically hurts right now. I can't…" Alex paused, then continued. "I won't go on living if she is dead. Life would be meaningless without Ariel."

"Don't talk that way," I snapped. "You can't think like that. Your life is precious. Besides, Ariel isn't dead. She is stronger than both of us. Ariel will be alive. Focus on that. Believe in that. We have to have hope, Alex. We have to believe she will be alive."

"I hope you're right," Alex said, his voice cracking. "Look at my hand." Alex raised his arm for me to inspect. His hand shook. "You see that. Fear. I'm deathly afraid of finding Ariel." He lowered his hand and turned his head away from me. "I have faced hordes of ruthless warriors. Yet, the risk of death has never bothered me. I have never felt such fear. But when I think of Ariel alone in the hands of the Abnormals, my body goes cold. I have never felt like this towards anyone, not even myself." Alex faced me again. "I love her so much, Jonas."

"I know. I'm afraid as well. But we can't give up. Hope. Alex.

We have to have hope," I said.

Alex nodded. "I will try."

CHAPTER 13 ARIEL

The cold night air burned against my bruised skin. Every part of me throbbed with pain as I took a ragged breath. How much longer can I keep this up? The sheer pleasure Vivienne took in burning me. Edric's laughter as he viciously attacked the burned skin. None of my training has prepared me for this. Death would be far simpler than enduring this torture.

Seven's sobs grew quieter. Ever since I have arrived, he has cried himself to sleep. For Seven, I had to be strong. He had to learn what it meant to face death. This was perhaps the last thing I would ever get to teach him. A tear slid down my face. I had such wonderful dreams. The life that I envisioned for Seven and I consisted of happiness. Sure, there would be days that we would be tired from working. But it would have been a good tired. A tired not from fighting and surviving. But a tired from working our land. A tired from keeping up a home. A real home full of family and friends was all I ever wanted. I wanted it more than the stars.

I stared up at those brilliant blinking lights as I remembered the nights not too long ago when I gazed up at them, dreaming that someday I would fly. So much has happened. My life had taken a path that I would never have dreamed of. Me, a Camp Freak, flew, became an Elite, then free. Free from the nightmares that had been my life. But, the best thing to ever happen to me was Seven. I will never forget the first day I saw him. A frightened little boy being robbed by Pick-axers. Gramps and I fought those thieves and res-cued Seven. Forever changing the path my life would take. An ac-tion that led me here to face a brutal death. I grinned. There isn't a thing I would change, not one.

A crunch of dried leaves drew my attention. My muscles stiff-ened as Vivienne approached me. She smirked, then sat down next to me.

"How was your day, little one?" She asked sweetly.

I sneered, "Lovely."

She laughed. "So much fight left in you. I respect your strength. Not many of your fellow Rebels still have your fire. Perhaps that drew me to you—that flame. I can't extinguish it, but I can make you burn. How much brighter will you burn in the coming days? What does your fury look like, I wonder?"

"If you want to see my rage, untie me, and I will show you," I smiled.

Vivienne laughed. "No. No. You are poison. Your fire is corruption, not purification. Not like real fire."

Vivienne ran her hand over the campfire letting the flames graze across her skin. "I was frightened of fire once. The Normals used it to burn my village. It consumed everything in its path. I only survived because of a sudden downpour of rain. Time passed, and I learned about the beauty of fire. Fire doesn't care who you are. It will burn you all the same. My fire, little one, my fire is unstoppable."

"Is it?" I questioned. "Do you know what I see, Vivienne?"

"Enlighten me," she grinned.

"I see no fire in you. I see nothing. Absolutely nothing. You rely on others to do your bidding, your killing. You attack children because they aren't strong enough to protect themselves against you. And when you see a real threat, you run to Edric or your crazed followers and cry for help. There is no fire inside of you. Only a coward resides in that void."

Her eyes widened, then slanted in rage. Vivienne raised her hand and slapped me across the face. I glared at her ignoring the pain.

"I don't fear you," I stated.

"What if I kill you?" She pulled out her knife and placed it on my neck. "Do you fear me now?"

I laughed. "No. I hold no fear of you. Kill me if you must, but know that I never feared you."

She lowered her knife, frowning deeply. "Why won't you beg me for your life? For a swift death?"

I didn't answer but returned her glare. She stood up and marched over to a bucket of water. Vivienne laughed as she threw the water onto the fire. Smoked filled the air as the warmth from the flames disappeared. Grinning with triumph, she walked over to me and leaned down. "I will make you beg before you die. Enjoy the lovely night air," she said in her sickly sweet voice.

The wind brushed against me, causing my muscles to clench in pain. And now, a deep cold started to grow. My body began to tremble. I laid my head down against the earth. Well, I made her mad. I smirked. It was something—a small win in this war I was doomed to fail.

****

Sunlight blurred my vision as I rolled onto my back. I groaned as my cold beaten body protested the movement. The Abnormals were slowly waking. The noise of food being cooked and people greeting each other began to fill the woods. I wonder what torture they had planned for us today?

Edric walked over to the extinguished fire and eyed me. He bent down and asked, "What happened?"

I raised an eyebrow at him. "What do you think?"

He looked back at the tent as if he could see Vivienne, then just grunted.

"You shouldn't make her angry. Why make this harder on yourself?"

I shrugged.

"For what it is worth, I'm sorry for how things turned out."

I frowned at him. He looked at me with eyes that were clear of anger and insanity.

"You saved my son and made a lot of sacrifices to do so. I'm grateful."

"Why?" I asked. "Why do this? Take Seven and get away from here. Start over. Why live this life?"

"For her," he said.

"Vivienne," I said in disgust.

He shook his head. "For my wife. The Normals took everything from me. Everything that was me is dead."

"You have gone too far!" I yelled. "Look at Seven. Your son is alive. Right there waiting for you to be his father, not a…."

He shot toward me and wrapped his fingers around my tattered shirt. "Not a creature of fire," he said, the insanity returned to his gaze.

"No," I said. "A monster."

He let go of me, then stood. "For your dedication to my son, for being his guardian, I promise that when your death comes, it will be swift. Until then," he said with malice in every word. "I will make you suffer every moment. I will make you regret becoming a Rebel."

Edric stormed off. Crazy! They were all insane! How did we not see this before we let them into our camp? Let them join us?

A young man with dark brown wings ran past me and into the tent. Their voices grew in excitement. Vivienne and Edric emerged, followed by the young man. Laughter bubbled from Vivienne as she neared me.

"You and your friends get a day of rest," she giggled. "We have found a beautiful little village not far from here. We don't want to be rude. We must say hello."

Bile rose in my throat as I knew exactly what they would do to that village. The Abnormals spent the morning preparing for the butchering of innocents. They gathered all of their warriors. A groan slipped from my lips as I saw them pull Red in with the group of warriors. His face was tight as he clenched his sword in his hands. I knew what horror he was about to witness and the choice he would be faced with. I turned my head from them. I couldn't watch as Vivienne and Edric shouted and encouraged their warriors. The loud roars from the Abnormals sounded more like a frenzy of released rage, from a pain so deep it would burn everything in its path.

The stomping of the Abnormal army echoed around me as they began their march. If only I could stop them. My eyes glanced down at the ropes tied around my hands and feet. I pulled against the restraints in a futile attempt to free myself. A cry of rage left me as they left the camp. Vivienne talked of fear. Edric and Vivienne will know fear if I ever get free.

CHAPTER 14 ARIEL

It was late in the night when the Abnormals marched back into camp. They cheered and raised their blood-soaked hands as they were welcomed back. They went to the river to wash while the ones that stayed behind started cooking. I heard a few cries as they dragged a woman by her hair. They flung her next to one of the Rebel warriors. Her sobs echoed through me, forcing me to turn away from the painful sight. Red came into view. Misery was etched onto his face, along with blood splattered across his chest. He glanced at me. Regret and pain filled his eyes. He turned his gaze from me and walked to the river.

Hushed voices caught my attention as the sobbing woman grew silent. I turned my body over to see what was happening. A knife! The woman had a knife. She cut one of the warriors free. A Dragon warrior pulled the ropes from his hands. The woman handed him the knife. He bent down to cut another warrior free. Another warrior stood, and then another. My heart leaped into my throat. All I could do was watch and hope they would go unnoticed.

"They are free!" I hear one of the Abnormals shout.

"Run!" I yelled at them.

They dashed into the woods. Fire burned behind them as the Abnormals chased after. In the chaos, I saw Red scramble into the air after them. I closed my eyes and waited. Sounds of battle cries and screams rang out, then soon it was quiet. They marched back. The woman was dragged back to camp, but this time lifeless. They brought back two of the warriors barely alive, but I didn't see the Dragon-man. Could he have escaped?

"Don't worry," Vivienne said as she wrapped her arm around Edric. They slowly walked back to their campsite. "Red will bring the other Rebel back."

"What if he doesn't?" Edric questioned.

"Then we know where his loyalties really lie," she answered.

The rest of the night was filled with horrible screams as the Abnormals tortured the two warriors. Tears ran down my face as they endured, then finally, painfully met death. It was hopeless. I will never get free, and none of my fellow Rebels will either. Death was the only way out of this prison. I let out a sigh. My breath could be seen as the air slowly grew colder. I hope Freckles and the girls are close to the Blue territory. They will be so happy to start building a home. I hope Jonas and Alex stay with them and live a life of peace. The thought of my dear family comforted my broken heart. At least they were safe and free. A slight smile made my lips curve. Focus on that, Ariel. Focus on what is good and happy. Remember, your family is still out there.

"He is back!" An Abnormal shouted.

Red marched back into camp and walked up to the fire where Edric and Vivienne sat. The fire danced over his stern features. His expression was so brutal. It was strange seeing him this way. He tossed something at their feet. I couldn't make out what it was.

"Proof of my loyalty to the Abnormals," Red stated. His voice was hard.

Edric picked up the lump of flesh, then handed it to Vivienne. A wide grin spread across her wicked face. She held the flesh up in the air. Then, I saw what it was. A hand. The hand of a Dragon-man. He wouldn't have given up his hand freely. The only way for the Dragon people to shoot their fire was through their hands. Without them, they cannot use their power.

"Is he dead?" Edric asked.

Red nodded.

"Good." Vivienne smiled, then tossed the hand into the fire. "You have proven yourself today, Red."

The smell of burning flesh filled my nose as I choked down the stench. Red shoulders stiffened as his eyes darted to mine, then quickly to Edric and Vivienne. They laughed at the exchange.

"Is it hard to stomach, Ariel?" Vivienne cooed. "Watching your friend's true nature be revealed. What is it like to know that you never really knew him?"

I glared at her, refusing to look at Red. Vivienne wouldn't see hatred or horror if she saw me look at him but remorse and sympathy. I know the hard choices that Red will have to continue to make to stay by Seven and protect him. Red had willingly sacrificed his heart in the hope of someday freeing Seven. He will never see anything but gratitude and empathy in my eyes. But that isn't what Vivienne must see. She must think that I am appalled and have turned my back on him if they are to trust Red. So, I glared at her and remained silent.

Edric chuckled. "I guess then you are truly one of us, now."

"Thank you," Red murmured, then walked away, disappearing into the darkness.

Vivienne and Edric laughed, then kissed each other. Edric raised his hand to her face pulling her closer. I averted my gaze to the fire and watched the Dragon warrior's hand slowly burn. The sacrifices that had been made today pushed down on my heart. Did the warrior give it up willingly to help Red continue his mission here? Or did Red have to kill him? Think of your family, Ariel. Think of their happiness. Tears blurred my vision as the smell of burnt flesh filled my nostrils.

How much will Seven have to endure before he is free? How long will it take Red to free him from this violence? Will it change Seven? I tried to think of my family's happiness, but the weight of my grief crashed down on me. Dark, painful thoughts raged through my mind. Is there any hope for Seven and Red to get free?

CHAPTER 15 JONAS

Four days! Four long unending days and no sight of the Abnormals' camp. We found their trail and followed it to the edge of a river. Then it split into two different paths. Frustrated, Michael ordered us to stop as he sent out scouts to survey each path. A Dragon-woman with bright, sunshine hair ran up to him. Her yellow eyes narrowed as she handed him a report.

"Thank you, Amanda." Michael unfolded the paper and read. "The trail hasn't ended on this side either?"

Amanda shook her head. "No."

"Go get something to eat and rest. Report back to me once you have finished." Michael ordered.

Amanda nodded and then left. Michael sighed as he sat down on a tree stump.

"What are you planning?" I asked.

"Time," Michael said, shaking his head. "The Abnormals know how to take away precious time and divide your forces. They know the need for us to hurry. I have two choices, and both I hate. Either we wait while I allow my scouts the time it will take to find the correct trail, then we march, or I divide my forces and attack them with half of my warriors. Either way, I will gamble lives. Ariel's life."

My body sunk to the ground, fear sapping my strength. "Which is the best choice?"

"I don't know," Michael whispered.

I glanced at him. The sleepless nights, the constant stress, and worry were engraved on his face.

"You need to sleep," I stated.

He looked at me, then back at the ground. "I can't. What I see in my dreams is far worse than being tired."

Silence fell between us. There was nothing for me to say. There was nothing I could say to make him sleep without seeing those awful images. They were the same images that plagued my sleep, images of death. Those nightmares were filled with sheer horror and pain. Waking up from them left me drained of all hope. Ariel's body broken, and her lifeless eyes staring up at the sky were all I saw when I closed my eyes. Every moment we marched and searched for them, we marched closer to her death and the death of all the captured Rebels.

"I keep hoping that Red left some sign. Some clue as to which path would lead us to them," Michael breathed. "So far, there has been none."

"I know Red is doing all he can to help," I said, trying to sound hopeful, forcing myself not to give up.

"What can he do?" Michael growled. "He is at their mercy. The moment he resists, they will kill him. He was sent to protect Seven and to be my spy. He can't face them alone. It will be suicide."

"Red is smart," I said. "He has grown up living in Camp 91. He knows how to survive surrounded by hostile people."

Michael nodded. "You're right. That is why I asked him to do this mission."

"We need to decide how to address this problem," I urged. "We cannot hesitate."

"I know. I know." Michael sat up and looked at me. "I'm struggling with controlling my personal feelings."

"Michael...,' I started, but he held up his hand.

"No need to chastise me." He gave me a small smile. "I'm in charge, and I need to get a grip on this situation. I can't save Ariel like this. So, I will control it because the alternative is not an option. She will be back with us, smiling again with Seven. I promise you, Jonas. I won't let us fail."

I placed my hand on his shoulder. "Thank you," I said, my voice sounding rough from the emotions that scraped down my throat.

Michael then headed off to talk to Simon. I took this moment to look for Alex. He was by the river letting his horse take a drink. He ran his hand down its neck repeatedly as he stared into the distance, lost in thought.

"Alex," I called out. He turned toward me, his facial expression somber. "I have heard from the second scout."

"And?" He asked, his voice tinged with desperation.

"The report is the same as the first. The trail continues."

He lowered his head. "The Abnormals know what they are doing."

"They do," I answered.

"What is Michael planning to do?"

"He has two plans, neither of them he likes," I said as I tossed a rock into the peaceful river.

Alex let out a deep breath. "Lose time but attack with the full might of our forces or divide our forces and save time, but attack with half of our strength."

I nodded.

"How many more days can Ariel last?" Alex turned toward me.

I swallowed. No answer came to me. It was all up to chance, to the whims of Edric and Vivienne. There was no way we could do more than we were at this moment, and that might not be enough to save any of the Rebels. What more could we do?

"I don't know how much hope there is left for me to hold on to," Alex murmured.

Shouts rose from the edge of our campsite. I could hear calls for a healer. Alex and I looked at each other, then ran to the source. There on the ground panting was a Dragon-man. Blood stained his body. His hand gripped tightly to his left wrist, that no longer had a hand. Burned marks covered the scarred flesh. I bent down next to him.

"You are safe," I said. "Who are you?"

"I'm Jason," he gritted out between clenched teeth. "I am a Rebel. The Abnormals kidnaped us."

Alex drew his attention as he abruptly asked, "Was Ariel there? Is she alive?"

His tired eyes looked up at him. "Yes. She was alive when I left."

Hope shone in Alex's eyes as he looked at me. I smiled. Alive. Ariel was still alive.

"How did you escape?" I asked.

Before he could answer, Tank pushed through the crowd and knelt next to him. He surveyed the burned wrist.

"We need to clean that, then seal it with fire," Tank said.

"I tried," Jason said. "But I passed out from the pain and couldn't do it properly."

"You did good," Tank smiled and placed his arms under his.

Tank helped Jason to his feet. Michael soon arrived and took in the situation.

"Will he be okay?" Michael asked Tank.

"Yes," Tank answered. "We just need to clean and seal the wound properly."

Michael turned his attention to Jason. "How did you get free?"

"A woman from one of the villages was dragged to the Abnormals' camp to be tortured. She snuck in a knife and cut me loose. I freed as many as I could before we had to run. I kept using my flames to hold them off. We fought and fought. There were so many of them. We knew that we couldn't fight our way out. Somebody had to make it back. They told me to run. The woman had fallen, and Abnormals were rushing for her. The two other warriors raced to her. I don't even know their names," Jason said.

He lowered his head as he fought back the physical and emotional pain. "I ran, but it wasn't long before a giant of a man confronted me. I prepared my fire and readied myself to fight. He dropped his sword and raised his hands. He said that his name was Red. He was Ariel's friend. It took me a moment, but I finally recognized him. He wanted me to show you how to find the Abnormals. I knew that if he went back to them without some sign that he had ended me, Red wouldn't be able to keep helping."

"Helping?" Michael asked.

"Michael," Tank interrupted. "We need to treat him."

"I can finish the report," Jason said.

Tank nodded.

"What happened after Red found you?" Michael asked.

"I recognized him. He was sneaking food and water to us. He looked over Ariel, but he couldn't help her as much as he did us. She was separated from us and placed next to the leader's tent. They have been giving Ariel special kinds of torture." Jason stopped, and he closed his eyes as if he saw those brutal events all over again. He took in a ragged breath, then finished. "I begged him to come with me, but he wouldn't leave the others and that little boy. So, I had to give him proof, my hand."

"Thank you," Michael said. "Once Tank has taken care of you, can you show us to the Abnormals' camp?"

Jason gave Michael a wrathful smile. "Gladly."

CHAPTER 16 ARIEL

The ground rushed up to my face as my arms collided with the dirt. The breath left my body. Pain throbbed down my shoulders. I rolled over. Vivienne covered her mouth with laughter that shook her. My head lay back on the ground. Dark clouds covered the sunrise. I was awakened to several kicks and punches before dawn. Today was the day, they had said. Seven stifled a cry as Edric dragged me to my feet. Please go. I pleaded in my head. Seven, please go away. Red moved silently next to Seven. We looked at each other for a moment. In his eyes, he was telling me goodbye. Then, he gently placed his hands on Seven's shoulders and started to lead him away from the horror that was about to befall the captured Rebels and me.

"Where are you going?" Vivienne asked, turning to face Red and Seven.

I held my breath. Please, let them leave.

"I'm taking Nathaniel into his tent," Red answered.

"No, no, no. That won't do," Vivienne said. "Bring my son next to me. He needs to watch how the enemy is dealt with. You are sweet, Red. But, the boy must grow up."

Red nodded and released Seven. Vivienne motioned for him to come to sit next to her on the log. Seven hesitantly walked over to her. She wrapped her around him and pulled Seven close to her.

"Now, you get to see the wonders that fire can do." A wicked smile spread slowly across her face. "It makes such beautiful music."

Smoke filled my nostrils. My breathing increased as panic rose in me. Then I heard it—the screams. Edric allowed me to spin around. The Rebels were not but a few feet from me. Fire burned around them as they sat on the straw. Abnormals started throwing sticks engulfed with flames at them, then laughing when one of them struck a person.

"No," I whispered. The air slowly filled with the stench of burning flesh. Tears burned my eyes. "No!" I screamed.

Rage flooded my body. I whipped around to see Edric's laughing face. My wrist being bound together didn't stop me from throwing my whole body into him. We fell to the ground. Clenching both of my hands into a fist, I hit Edric over and over, screaming at him. Two sets of hands dragged me off of him. Edric stood. Blood ran down his face. He glared at me. Edric raised his fist then slammed it across my cheek. The two men released me, allowing me to fall back to the ground.

"What have you done?" Vivienne yelled.

All eyes turned to her. She stood staring at the Rebels. My gaze shifted to see what had surprised her. A smile formed on my lips. Red stood next to the dying fire. An empty wooden bucket lay at his feet. Some of the Rebels' hair dripped with water.

"Traitor," Vivienne hissed.

Red looked at me. "I'm sorry. I couldn't watch this and do nothing."

Men pushed Red over to me. Vivienne stomped over to us.

"I knew it," Vivienne fumed. "I knew you were never one of us."

Red grinned.

Edric's frown deepened. "How should we punish him, my love?"

Vivienne crossed her arm. "I know how to hurt him." Laughter bubbled from her. "This will be even better. Tie Red up and bring them both over to that log." Vivienne pointed.

Red arms were tied behind his back, and then we were dragged next to Seven. Vivienne whispered in Edric's ear. Soon, Edric's laughter filled the camp.

"Excellent," Edric said. "Begin whenever you are ready."

Vivienne reached down and dragged me close to the fire. She smiled down at me. I took a deep breath preparing myself for the pain. Vivienne ripped up my tunic, revealing my stomach. She picked up a stick from the fire with her other hand. Vivienne waved the flame in front of my face. Laughing, she placed the fire on my stomach. Pain seared through me. Blood filled my mouth as I bit down on my lip, keeping down my scream. She raised the fire off of my stomach. The wind hurt as it blew across the damaged skin. Then, Vivienne lowered it again, pressing harder on the same spot. I squeezed my eyes shut. Sweat poured down my face. Then I heard footsteps running toward me.

"Stop it!"

I opened my eyes to find Seven. He pushed Vivienne away as he rushed past her. Shock and disgust filled her face.

"Stop it!" Seven yelled. "I won't let you hurt her."

"Go," I moaned. "Seven run!"

Seven bent down and pulled my head on top of his knees. "I won't leave you."

Vivienne shrugged, then tossed the stick back into the fire. Edric rushed over and pulled Seven away from me.

"You need to learn our ways!" Edric shouted.

"I will never learn your ways! They are horrible. You murder people! You are killing my guardian! Father! She saved me, and you are killing her," Seven cried.

Edric yanked Seven away and shoved him down onto the log. "Sit there and don't move."

Vivienne walked over to Edric. "It is okay, my love. We all understand. It will take time for him to learn. His mind was poisoned against you."

"It is time for the source of that poison to die," Edric gritted out.

"Indeed." Vivienne smiled, then walked over to me. "Time to die, sweet little Camp Freak."

A large man dragged me over to Edric. They sat me up facing them. My heart pounded hard against my chest. This was it—the end. I looked at Seven. Tears flowed down his face. I smiled at him, and then I faced Edric. I will not look away from death.

"Bring Red here," Edric ordered.

The same large man forced **Red** to stand next to Edric. With one swift movement, Edric cut **Red**'s hands free. Then, he handed him the sword. Red frowned at him.

"You have one chance to redeem yourself," Edric said. "Kill Ariel."

Red eyes widened. "No."

Vivienne smiled. "Then who will watch over Nathaniel or, as you like to call him, Seven. Isn't that what you promised Ariel?"

Red looked down at me. I nodded at him. This was for the best. Red would live and be able to protect Seven and save him from this madness.

"I can't," Red said.

"Yes, you can," I said. "I'd rather die by your hands than theirs."

Red nodded slowly. He walked and stood behind me. "Don't look," he whispered.

I turned my head away from him and waited. The sword whistled as it cut through the air. As the weapon swooshed down toward me, I took my last breath.

Thud!

The sword crashed down on the ground cutting the ropes around my hands and wings. I jumped up and stared at Red.

"We go out together," he said.

"Together, then." I nodded.

"Guardian!" Seven yelled as he ran toward us, dragging a sword with him.

"Grab him!" Vivienne shouted.

"Don't touch him," Edric ordered.

Everyone froze, obeying Edric's command. Vivienne frowned at him. Edric's eyes followed Seven as he walked over to Red and me.

"Nathaniel," Edric said. "You have a choice to make. One that will determine the outcome of your life. You can either give that sword to Ariel or me. You have lived with both of us. You know how our lives are. Nathaniel, you need to choose what you want for your future. Nathaniel, give me the sword, and you will live a long life. It will be hard. Lessons like these are hard to learn. Life shouldn't be this way for a child. But you are no longer a child. The day that our village was destroyed, so was your childhood. I see a man before me. A man must decide if he wants to live or die. For you will surely die if you give that sword to Ariel. She has no future. Death is coming for her, and it will be by my hands. Nathaniel, give me the sword."

"You fool!" I yelled. "Seven is a child! How can you make him choose between two people he loves? Just take the sword from him and take him away from this."

"You are wrong," Edric stated. "He is old enough to choose his life."

"You are a cruel man. This is your son!" I argued.

"Nathaniel, choose now. Give me the sword, son." Edric held his hand out toward Seven.

I looked down at Seven. He stood calmly as he faced his father.

"Give him the sword, Seven. I love you. Please, give him the sword," I begged.

Seven looked up at me, grabbed my hand, and placed the sword in my palm. My fingers wrapped around the hilt. Tears blurred my vision as I looked at Seven.

"We are in this together," Seven said.

I nodded.

"You are no longer my son," Edric seethed. "You will die as my enemy."

"You will not lay a hand on Seven," I voiced as my fingers tightened around the hilt.

With my free hand, I moved Seven between Red and me. We each stood back to back, protecting Seven. Our wings stretched out, swords raised. Death was coming, but it was in for a fight.

"Let's show these Abnormals how good Elite are," Red said.

I smiled. "Agreed."

CHAPTER 17 ARIEL

"Kill them," Edric said as he pointed to two large Abnormals.

They nodded, unsheathed their swords, then marched towards us. Red spread his legs apart, securing his balance. I squeezed Seven's shoulder.

"Stay behind us," I said.

Seven nodded, then crouched down to his knees. Our opponents smirked, then split. One with long hair moved to face Red. At the same time, the one with blond hair eyed me.

"Make them suffer!" Edric yelled.

The blond warrior charged. He swung his sword low aiming for my waist. My sword caught his. His sword slid down mine. He smirked, then he aimed it toward Seven. Using my shoulder, I shoved him sideways. He threw out his hands, losing his balance. The blonde warrior fell. He waved at me to come at him. I shook my head.

The warrior sighed, then stood. He was testing me. He spread his wings out and jumped into the air. He let out a yell and charged me from the sky. The speed at which he flew would make this hard to block. I raised my sword sideways, using my free hand to balance the blade. I waited. Closer. Just a little closer. The blonde warrior's sword was about to strike mine. Using his force against him, I titled my sword and moved my body out of his path. His blade slid down mine. The warrior's eyes widened as my hilt smashed into the side of his face. He fell at Seven's feet. With one swift movement, I plunged the sword through his back. He screamed, then blood poured out of his body.

Red had made quick work of his opponent. We regrouped and formed our protective stance around Seven. Edric growled and pointed to more of his warriors. We were surrounded. The warriors approached from both sides. Red and I worked together, defending each other. We moved closer as they pressed us. Seven's hands rested on the back of my calves. I could feel his hands shaking. Not today. Seven will not die today.

A cry of anger burst from my lungs as I used my wings to push the two men back. Quickly, I ran at them. Shocked, they tried to block. I slid across the grass, cutting one of the men's knees. He fell to the ground. My leg kicked out, slamming into the back of the other warrior's calf. He struggled to keep his balance. Using his loss of focus against him, I jumped up and rammed my sword through the back of his neck. Blood gurgled from his throat as he sank to the ground. The second warrior waved his hands up at me.

"No, please," he begged.

I frowned, then ran back to Red and Seven. Edric marched over to the wounded man.

"Coward," he shouted, then he killed him.

My mouth dropped. He killed his own warrior. What kind of man does that? I turned my attention back to the battle. Red swung his sword, slicing through one of Abnormal's stomach. In the corner of my eye, I caught sight of a warrior swinging his weapon toward Red's neck. Turning, I brought my sword up and blocked his attack. Red glanced up, and then without hesitation, he made a killing blow. Red and I nodded at each other. Then, we formed our protective stance around Seven again.

Edric glared at us. "All of you will die!"

"Well, they took their time," Red said, then started laughing.

I turned to see what had driven my friend to break. Horses rushed into the clearing. Warriors sat on top of them, yelling a battle cry. The Rebels! Red turned to me with a smile on his face. I returned the smile.

"Not today," I said.

Red grinned. "Not today."

Red and I let out our own battle cries with renewed energy, then flew into action. Abnormals swarmed us as Edric shouted out commands. It wasn't long before Rebels stood by our sides. A wave of fire rushed around us. Tank! He was the first to find us. Soon, the others came. Abnormals took to the sky and flew down at us. Tank used his fire to prevent them from getting too close, while Sy used a bow to pick off those who got through.

An Abnormal rushed us, aiming for Sy. Her focus was on the sky. I jumped behind her just as the Abnormal swung down their sword. My blade caught theirs. Undaunted by my sudden appearance, the warrior punched with his free hand. His fist crashed down on my already broken nose. Blood squirted out from the barely healed wound. The blow caused my vision to go dark for a terrifying moment. I shook my head. Once I regained my vision, the warrior lay dead at my feet. Alex stood next to me. Pure hatred etched on his face.

"Alex," I breathed.

He turned to me. His dark eyes were like a storm.

"Thank you," I said.

He nodded and then moved to stand at my side. Another wave rushed us. And another. Edric approached, yelling at his men to target Alex and me. In the distance, Michael kicked his horse into a gallop. He raced toward Edric. Michael jumped off his horse and tackled Edric to the ground as soon as he was close. They rolled on the dirt, each of them punching the other. Michael scrambled to his feet. He raised his hands as his eyes glowed with his power.

Vivienne jumped on his back. Michael lost his balance and fell to the ground. Edric stood and withdrew his blade. My heart stopped. No! My feet broke out into a run. Michael threw Vivienne off of him. She started to claw at him. Edric grinned as we walked over to them. Vivienne screamed at Michael to keep his attention on her.

"Michael!" I yelled. "Behind you!"

Michael looked up at me, then within an instance, his eyes glowed, and a bright blue wave of power shot out behind him. The wave knocked Edric to the ground. Michael pinned Vivienne. She quickly surrendered.

"Are you okay?" I asked as I reached him.

"Yes," Michael said.

I turned to Edric. He fumed at me as he stood.

"You will die today, Camp Freak! Abomination!" Edric yelled. "The Abnormals are warriors of justice. We will not be defeated today."

"Justice?" I questioned. "Vengeance is more accurate. You call Alex a butcher, but you butcher anyone that believes differently than you. That is not justice."

Edric laughed. "No, but it does sound better when winning more fodder to my army."

"Come then," I gritted out. "Let's finish this."

"Gladly," Edric smiled.

He ran at me, then jumped in the air. Edric extended out his leg, kicking me right in the chest. The impact sent me sprawling. He dropped down, stomping on my leg. Edric laughed as he jumped back into the air. I rolled over to my side. Edric flew down low, swinging his sword toward me. My blade clung off of his as I blocked the strike. Again, he flew toward me, waving his sword. This time, I dodged the attack, then jumped in the air. I grabbed his feet and pulled him as I let my body fall to the ground. We both collided into the dirt with a loud thud.

Quickly standing, I moved into a fighting stance. Edric pushed himself off the ground. He frowned at me, then bolted straight toward me. I dodged, but I wasn't fast enough. As my body moved out of his path, Edric grabbed my shirt, pulling me off my feet. My back hit the hard ground. Edric sat on me. He laughed loudly, then proceeded to punch me. I raised my arms to protect my face from his attacks.

"Father!" Seven's voice echoed over Edric's laughter.

Edric stopped and looked at his son. Seven stood with his shoulders squared as he faced his father. His face was wet from crying. Seven took in a deep breath.

"Stop this. Please. This is not you. You asked me to choose. Well, now I'm asking you to choose. I want you to choose me. Please, stop this and choose me," Seven pleaded.

Edric looked down at me, then back up to Seven. "I'm not that man anymore. He died in our village. The fire burned his soul from this body. All that is left is the need to kill and destroy. I can't turn back."

"Yes, you can!" Seven yelled. "It isn't too late. Please, Father."

A deep sigh escaped Edric's lips. "No. Now you better run because you are next to die."

Fury exploded through me as I jumped up from the ground catching him off guard. I stood in front of Seven.

"I don't want to kill you," I stated. "You are Seven's father, but I will end you if you threaten his life one more time."

Edric's smile widened as a crazed expression flooded his features. "I will burn everyone! I will watch as the flesh melts off your bones. And…" he paused as his eyes shifted to Seven. "and Nathaniel's. Betrayal doesn't sit well with me, boy!"

"You will never touch him!" I shouted.

My feet pushed me off the ground as I sprang into the sky. I came down hard, sword slashing through the air. Our blades clanged loudly against each other. Edric fought with wild abandon as I defended against his attacks. I watched and waited. Soon he would have an opening. There! I jammed my sword through his waist. In return, he brought his blade down, slashing my right arm.

My wings spread out, and I flew back, giving myself some room to recover. Hot sticky blood ran down my arm. I raised my sword, preparing for his next onslaught. He held his waist. Something in his eyes changed as he looked at Seven. He frowned, then turned his focus back on me. Edric let out a battle cry and then sprinted toward me. I braced. He brought his sword out to his side, going for a broad attack aiming for my sword arm this time. This move left his chest open. Taking the opportunity, I struck. My blade plunged deep into his chest. He fell to the ground. My eyes widened when I noticed that he wasn't going for my arm. He threw his sword away. It laid on the ground close to a weeping Vivienne.

I turned to him. "Why?" I asked.

He smiled up at me. "For Nathaniel's future."

Seven ran toward him and fell to the ground next to him. His body shook with tears.

"Father!" He cried. "Father!"

Edric raised a bloodied hand onto Seven's head. "Will you ever forgive me?" Then, Edric's head rolled to the side. His eyes stared lifelessly at Vivienne.

"No!" Seven screamed. "Father! Why?"

I bent down and laid my hand on Seven's back. He turned and wrapped his arms around my stomach.

"Why didn't he choose me?" Why did he do this?" Seven shouted.

"I don't know," I whispered. "But in the end, Seven, he chose you."

Seven froze, then looked up at me. "He did?"

I nodded.

"You!" Vivienne cried out. She picked up Edric's sword. Her red hair blew furiously around her. "You destroyed my army. My life! You killed the man I loved! You took away my chance at greatness. I will enjoy killing you."

She charged at me. I jumped to my feet, blocking her sword with mine. Seven scrambled behind me. Vivienne screamed, then lashed out. Every blow, my blade stopped with ease. As she swung her sword to the side, I slashed my weapon down on hers, hitting it with all my strength. The sword fell onto the dirt. It was over. Vivienne screamed and fell to the ground. She covered her face as her body shook.

"Please don't kill me," Vivienne whimpered. "Please."

I gritted my teeth. The rage inside me wanted nothing more than to end this vile woman. This woman attacked and brutally murdered innocents. This woman scarred Elizabeth. This woman who took Seven from me! My fingers tightened around my hilt. I glared down at her. Gramps' face flashed in my mind. Gramps showed endless kindness in the face of hatred as he repeatedly showed mercy to the Pickaxers that tormented us. Then, I saw Jonas's troubled face as he told me of the burdens he had suffered when he denied mercy. I took a deep breath. No. I will not give in to my anger. My sword lowered.

"I never want to see you again," I demanded.

"Never," Vivienne squeaked out. "I promise."

I turned my back toward her and walked to Seven.

"Are you okay," I asked.

Seven wiped his eyes. "I'm going to miss him."

"I know," I whispered.

"Guardian," Seven said. "Will you be my mother again?"

I smiled. "I never stopped."

Seven wrapped his arms around my neck and pulled me in for a hug. Michael ran up to us. He held his hand to me. I placed my hand in his, and he pulled me off the ground.

"Sorry, I left. Battle drew me away. I think that was their intent." Michael frowned.

"Is it over?" I asked, looking around at the Abnormals. All of them had sunk to their knees, staring at their fallen leader.

Michael sighed. "It is over."

I turned back to him. "Thank you for coming to save us."

Michael's eyes met mine. I could feel myself being pulled toward him. He raised his hands and cupped my face.

"There you are!" Jonas exclaimed.

Michael stepped back, then smiled at me. Soon arms pulled me into a tight hug. Pain shot down my right arm.

"Ow," I said, laughing

Jonas pulled back and looked at my wounds. "Sorry," he said. "I'm just so relieved."

Seven jumped up, and Jonas quickly caught him and hugged him tightly. "Both of you are alive. We had feared the worst."

I hugged Jonas and Seven. "My family." I smiled.

Soon, we were joined by Sy and Tank. Seven and I were pulled from one hug to another. Red found us, and to his surprise, he was attacked with hugs. Laughter bellowed out of Red.

"You came just in time," Red said. "It wasn't looking good for us."

I frowned. "No."

"You two sure gave them a fight, though," Tank stated.

Red smirked. "Did you doubt that we would?"

Sy laughed. "Never!"

Joy flooded me. It was over. This horrible nightmare was over. Alex came up to us. Blood covered his face. I reached for him. My hand ran across his cheek as I surveyed him.

"Are you hurt?" I asked.

Alex shook his head. "Not my blood."

I breathed out a sigh of relief. Then without warning, Alex wrapped his arms around me and squeezed me tightly. He brought his mouth down to my ear and whispered. "I thought I lost you." My left arm raised up his back as I returned the hug. "You don't know how much that tormented me."

I pulled out of his grasp. "You came for me," I said. "Thank you."

"I will always come for you," Alex said quietly, turning away.

"Wait," I said.

He stopped and looked back at me.

"Where are you going?" I asked.

He smiled. "I will be back." Alex pointed at the Rebels. "I am going to help Michael round up the rest of these animals."

I nodded. "I will help."

"No. You won't," ordered Sy. "Your arm needs to be looked at, and you have done enough. It is time for you to rest. We didn't ride out here to save you, only to let you die from exhaustion."

"But," I argued.

Sy raised her finger at me and glared. "But nothing." Then she pointed to Tank. "Go over to him so he can look at your wounds."

I sighed, then smiled.

Jonas laughed. "Come on, Ariel. Let's get you patched up."

I nodded, then shrugged at Alex. He smiled at me.

"Get some rest. I will be there soon," he said, then walked toward Michael.

Sy pulled me along with her. Tank suggested that we go over to one of the wagons they had brought. Seven held my hand as we all walked side by side. My heart was overwhelmed with the joy that filled it. Here beside me was my family. People that would risk their lives for me. People who I would die for. We had survived the Camps. And now we had survived the Abnormals. We were free to start our dream.

I shook my head as I remembered my last thoughts on freedom. There was so much more to it. It was complicated. Freedom is hard and full of pain and loss. But, freedom is also full of love and joy. It is full of friends and family. And sometimes. Sometimes. Dreams do come true.

Epilogue

CHAPTER 18 ALEX

It was simple. The Abnormals lost all their desire to fight once their leader lay dead. A few wanted to push back against Michael's offer of peace. I enjoyed pushing them right back into the dirt. They were cowards. They used the fear of fire as a weapon. They lack any actual skill or any true devotion to a cause. Michael gave them a choice to put this behind them and come with us to the Blue Territory or be brought there as prisoners. Most chose to give up. There weren't many that we had to tie up.

Michael was putting all of us at risk by trusting these animals. It was his homeland. I don't care what he does. I will protect my family. That word made me pause my movements. Family. A small smile pulled at my lips. Ariel gave me that. Just thinking of her made my body feel lighter. The weight of my past seemed to slip away. Never has anyone made me feel this way. And no one will take it away.

My eyes found the target. Vivienne. She broke Ariel's heart. She tortured Ariel. My fists clenched. Vivienne tried to kill Ariel. A fire of hatred consumed me like never before. When those men attacked us in that Normal village, it angered me, but her. Vivienne has awakened a beast inside of me. Vivienne is nothing more than a vile creature. A creature that has hurt the woman who holds my heart. The beast inside me can only be satisfied with the death of that vile creature.

I took my time walking over to her. Vivienne spotted me. Fear shone brightly in her eyes. None of the Rebels noticed her. They were too busy helping the victims that survived their torture. Many of them had burn marks on their skin. Some of them didn't survive the battle. Vivienne pulled at the ropes that bound her hands. Her breathing came out in loud gasps as my fingers curled around the ropes at her wrists.

"What are you doing?" Vivienne whimpered.

I said nothing as I pulled her alongside me. The Rebels began marching the Abnormals back into the woods. Soon, they would be leaving. This was the perfect opportunity to settle things with Vivienne. I led us across the clearing. A large river wildly cut through the grassy field. Several large rocks sat along the river's bank. Vivienne started to dig her nails into my hands.

"Take me back to the Rebels!" She demanded.

I grinned at her. "You won't see the Rebels again."

Vivienne yanked her arm, desperately trying to free herself. Laughter sprung from my mouth at her pathetic effort.

"I'll scream," Vivienne threatened.

"You can," I said. "You can also die very slowly."

Vivienne's face drained of all its color. "Why?"

I raised my eyebrow at her, then turned away. She didn't deserve an answer to such a ridiculous question. Why? She was the tormentor of the only person I love. Once we reached the riverbank, I shoved her down on one of the large rocks. Her body

trembled.

"Please spare me," Vivienne begged.

I laughed. "Why would I do that?"

"Ariel," Vivienne said. "Ariel spared me."

I frowned.

Vivienne took my silence as an encouragement to continue.

"You are in love with her. I can tell. What would she think of you

if you killed me after she let me live? How would she see you?

Your sweet Ariel. What will she see if you murder me? A butcher,

perhaps."

I glanced down at my hands, my mind racing. Would Ariel

hate me?

"Do you see the blood that stains your hands?" Vivienne

asked. "Will you taint your precious Ariel with those hands?"

My fingers clenched tightly together. Blood from this battle

still covered me. I closed my eyes. Scenes of many battles ran through my mind. Conrad's voice commanding me to take more lives echoed in my ears. How much blood have I washed from these hands? Was it too much to hope that a man like me could be with someone like her?

"Take me back," Vivienne said, her voice shaking as she tried to take control of me.

My eyes opened as I looked at this conniving creature before me. Conrad had told me that Ariel couldn't make the hard choices. Her conscience wouldn't let her. Ariel needed someone to make sure that her kindness didn't betray her. A partner that would bloody his soul to keep hers free from the guilt. Conrad trained me to be that partner. To protect her no matter the cost to my own mind. I had hated him for molding me into a tool for his brat. Then, I met her. Ariel was like no one I have ever seen. So much life. So much strength. Hope shone in her eyes despite what she had gone through. Ariel accepted me, knowing who I am. Without hesitation.

I pulled out the small dagger Ariel had given me from my belt. It would be perfect for this task. For once, I'm glad I was trained to become this beast. There is nothing in this world that I wouldn't do to keep my family safe.

"What..what..are you doing?" Vivienne's body trembled as she tried to stand.

I grabbed her shoulder, digging my fingers deep into her skin. A cry escaped her as I pushed her back down. Slowly bending down to look her in the eyes, I grinned.

"I'm keeping a promise to a little girl," I answered.

The knife reflected the light from the sun as it rested on her neck. Tears ran down her face.

"Please, please. Please don't kill me," Vivienne cried. "I don't want to die."

I leaned in close to her ear. Vivienne's body shook as I spoke.

"Then you should have never hurt Ariel."

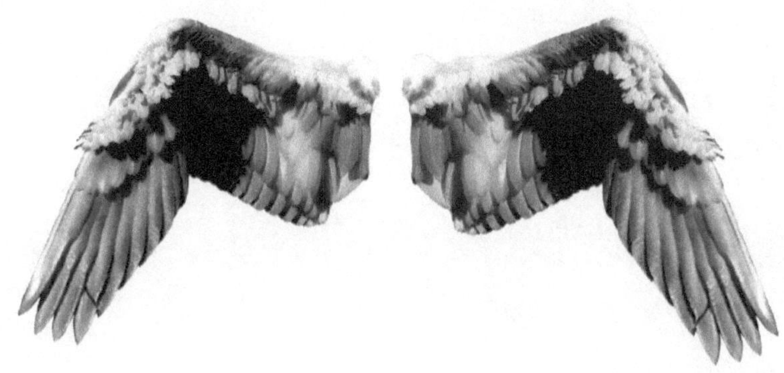

AUTHOR'S NOTE

Thank you so much for reading and supporting the series.

To stay up-to-date on my projects and the Freaks series, follow my Facebook page or my Instagram @j.o.young.

https://www.facebook.com/TheFreaksBookSeries

Please consider leaving a review. It helps people find my books.

Thank you for the support!

ABOUT THE AUTHOR

J. O Young lives in Oklahoma with her comic books enthusiast husband, heroic chihuahua, Shazam, and an excitable miniature schnauzer, Ewok. By day, she is a teacher. By night, she writes, reads anything from comics to science fiction and fantasy novels, and can be found at comic shops, books stores, and libraries.

www.ingramcontent.com/pod-product-compliance
Lightning Source LLC
Chambersburg PA
CBHW030322160726

47992CB00005B/2129

9 798826 530696